I0745251

PRAISE FOR IRIS MORLAND

THE PRINCE I LOVE TO HATE

The Prince I Love To Hate is an absolute must read! This romcom will have you rooting for Niamh and Olivier right from their hilarious first meeting.

— HARLEQUIN BOOK JUNKIE BLOG

OOPSIE DAISY

Quirky, fun, witty, hilarious! Iris Morland always manages to get me to laugh out loud.

— WHISPERING CHAPTERS

HE LOVES ME, HE LOVES ME NOT

A hilarious, sexy and heartwarming romantic comedy...you do not want to miss this fun, feel-good romance.

— MARY DUBÉ, CONTEMPORARILY EVER AFTER

...refreshing, funny, emotionally charged, and very entertaining to read.

— CAROL, TIL THE LAST PAGE

There is humor, there is heart and there is heat in this story! I absolutely loved it! . . . Mari and Liam delivered. Yowza, their chemistry was palpable.

— BIBLIOPHILE CHLOE

Petal Plucker

Funny, charming, and utterly captivating! I devoured this sparkling read.

— ANNIKA MARTIN, NEW YORK TIMES BESTSELLING AUTHOR

Petal Plucker was funny, entertaining, fresh and fan-yourself-worthy . . . Their enemies-to-lovers romance is both charming, tender and steamy, and you'll love both of these characters (and their families!) and their sigh-worthy happily ever after.

— MARY DUBÉ, CONTEMPORARILY EVER AFTER

Morland has created a masterpiece of a romance . . . one of my favorite [books] of the year.

— CRISTIINA READS

Humorous, raunchy, and refreshing, Petal Plucker has rightfully earned its way, in my opinion, as one of the best romantic comedy [books] this year.

— CAROL, TIL THE LAST PAGE

My One and Only

This book was gripping, well written & the chemistry between the characters sizzled throughout this wonderful read.

— AMAZON REVIEW

All I Want Is You

Another heartfelt, steamy, terrific story. This is an author who really knows how to create a story that catches a reader's attention and characters that capture her heart.

— BOOKADDICT

TAKING A CHANCE ON LOVE

Thea and Anthony are in for a surprise when it comes to the language of the heart . . . I am in awe.

— HOPELESS ROMANTIC BLOG

THEN CAME YOU

This story really pulled all my heartstrings. This was truly a beautiful story and makes you believe there really is true love out there.

— MEME CHANELL BOOK CORNER

ALSO BY IRIS MORLAND

THE HEIR AFFAIR DUET

The Prince I Love to Hate

The Princess I Hate to Love

HERON'S LANDING

Say You're Mine

All I Ask of You

Make Me Yours

Hold Me Close

THE FLOWER SHOP SISTERS

War of the Roses

Petal Plucker

He Loves Me, He Loves Me Not

Oopsie Daisy

LOVE EVERLASTING

including

THE YOUNGERS

Then Came You

Taking a Chance on Love

All I Want Is You

My One and Only

THE THORNTONS

The Nearness of You

The Very Thought of You

If I Can't Have You

Dream a Little Dream of Me

Someone to Watch Over Me

Till There Was You

I'll Be Home for Christmas

THE PRINCESS I HATE TO LOVE

THE HEIR AFFAIR DUET

IRIS MORLAND

BLUE VIOLET PRESS LLC

This book is a work of fiction. The names, characters, places and incidents are products of the writer's imagination or have been used fictitiously and are not to be constructed as real. Any resemblance to persons, living or dead, actual events, locales or organizations is entirely coincidental.

The Princess I Hate to Love
Copyright © 2021 by Iris Morland
Published by Blue Violet Press LLC
Seattle, Washington

Cover design by Qamber Designs

All rights reserved. No part of this book may be reproduced in any form or by any electronic or mechanical means, including information storage and retrieval systems, without written permission from the author, except for the use of brief quotations in a book review.

To Poppy and Clementine, for always providing inspiration for cat characters in my books.

THE PRINCESS I HATE TO LOVE

CHAPTER ONE

When I imagined my wedding night, I never expected that I'd be standing outside my beloved wife's bedroom door, pounding on it to let me inside.

"You can't avoid me forever!" I pounded my fist one last time against the expensive wood.

"Of course I can. Have you seen this place? It's fucking huge!"

I heard what sounded like rustling. I closed my eyes, leaning my forehead against the door. I'd imagined helping Niamh out of her wedding dress, but here I was, a dog barking at the door to be let in.

"Niamh," I said, forcing calm into my voice. "We need to talk."

"There's nothing to talk about. I'm tired. Go away."

I growled. I jiggled the knob, but it stayed firmly locked. Someone cleared their throat behind me, and I turned to see my secretary Arthur Laurent, who was studiously avoiding looking at the locked door.

"Would you like me to procure the key from Madam

LeRoux, Your Highness?" he asked in French. While I spoke English solely with my American bride, I rarely spoke it to anyone inside the palace.

"And have the entire palace know my wife has locked me out on our wedding night? No, thank you." I noticed the dark circles under Laurent's eyes. Ever the professional, he'd never complained when I'd dropped the bombshell of my sudden engagement, subsequent marriage, and the creation of a new princess of Salasia into his lap. But if I hadn't slept, he hadn't, either.

"Go to bed, Laurent. I'll take care of this," I said.

Laurent leaned back on his heels. "There is a way inside."

Right then, I was glad Niamh couldn't understand our conversation. I smiled for the first time in hours. "Is there?"

"Yes. The door that adjoins your chambers—the lock, it is, shall we say…" Laurent stared at the ceiling. "Very old."

Since I'd lived in my own apartments in another part of the palace until I'd moved into the East Wing last week, I didn't know the ins and outs of its layout. Laurent, though, having worked at the palace for over twenty years, he knew.

I clapped him on the shoulder. "You're my favorite servant, you know that?"

"So you've said, despite my lack of holiday for over a decade."

Laurent never wanted to go on holiday anyway. I gave him a droll look, shooing him off to sleep. Before he left, though, he said quietly, "Be gentle with her, sir. She's young and in a strange place."

My frustration with Niamh melted. I sighed. "I won't say that you're correct."

"Of course not, sir. That would be out of character." Laurent bowed, and I dismissed him for the night.

I entered my own chambers. Opulent and limned with gold, the curtains blood red and velvet, embroidered with the royal carnation, it looked like something out of eighteenth-century Versailles.

Which was precisely the point: when it was built, my long-dead ancestors had attempted to copy the court of Louis XIV, although luckily for them, they'd avoided the later years involving guillotines and rolling heads. Apparently, they hadn't been creative enough to come up with their interior designs.

Although there had been updates to the bedding, draperies, and carpets since then, they'd always kept a similar style. I had to admit, I'd never liked the opulence. I understood that a palace should look like a palace and not some university flat with broken-down furniture from IKEA, but there had to be a happy medium between the two.

My bedroom was connected to another room, a parlor, that connected to Niamh's bedroom. Entering it, I took in the uneaten tray of dinner that Niamh hadn't touched. Going to the other door, I remembered another door in my previous apartments that was similarly old. Pushing against it with my shoulder, I was able to unlatch the lock before turning the knob.

I opened the door to find Niamh desperately trying to undo the countless tiny buttons down the back of her wedding dress. She whirled at my entrance, her eyes as wide as saucers.

"What the fuck! How did you—"

"Do you need help?"

With her long, dark hair coiled about her head and pearls surrounding her slender throat, she was the complete opposite of the ragamuffin girl I'd first encountered at her grandfather's estate in Dublin. On our journey through Europe, she'd always worn jeans, sneakers, and a hoodie when it was cold. I'd seen her wear mascara once.

Now, though, she wore an ivory gown that accentuated her curves. It was made of silk and beaded with thousands of crystals down the back and along the train and around the neckline. Sleeves came to her elbows. Although she'd worn a veil in the church, she'd already taken it off.

"You look beautiful," I said softly.

"Yes, I know. I look like a princess."

Her words had an edge to them. I was fairly certain if I approached too quickly, she'd gouge my eyes out.

She had a reason to hate me, of course. I'd forced her into this marriage. Because I wanted to keep the secret of my bastardy a secret. Because I wanted to remain the Hereditary Prince of Salasia, the heir to the Valady Dynasty. I wasn't about to let over three hundred years of my family ruling this small principality crumble with me.

So, Niamh, the true heir to the throne after her older brother Liam, was my ticket to holding onto my birthright. She'd only agreed to marry me because she didn't want to ruin her brother's life. She was extremely protective of him, sometimes to the point that I wondered if there was another reason why.

"We agreed that we would spend the night together," I said, "so as not to risk gossip starting."

"I changed my mind."

She sat down at a vanity and began to take off her

jewelry. I barely restrained myself from throttling her, but I remembered Laurent's words. *Be gentle with her, sir. She's young and in a strange place.*

"I'm trying to protect you," I said.

She looked at me from the mirror. "Really? Because I'm fairly certain everything you've done has been to protect yourself, dearest husband."

I leaned over her, my hands now on her upper arms. We gazed at our reflections.

"You agreed to this marriage. You had ample time to change your mind. Don't act as if I chained you up in a dungeon to get you to agree. Besides." I trailed my hands down her arms, enjoying feeling her shiver. "It's not as if there isn't chemistry here." I kissed the side of her neck. I saw her close her eyes.

"You know very well why I said yes. But if you think I'm going to be your little dutiful wife who only ever nods her head, you're very mistaken."

I tilted her chin up so she looked me in the eyes. "I never expected anything else."

Heat crackled between us. We'd barely touched since our engagement three months ago. We'd kissed after we'd said our vows at the royal chapel. But now, we were finally alone, and the memory of the last time we'd been in that hotel room in Berlin, when I'd made her come under my tongue, sent a thrill through my body. My cock hardened instantly.

"I'm not going to have hate sex with you," she whispered.

I laughed. I didn't tell her I didn't believe her. Instead, I began to unbutton her dress. With each patch of pale skin revealed, I could hear her breathing increase. A flush had begun to crawl from her chest into her face. She could deny this attraction between us until her dying day. Her body told a different story.

Finally, the gown unbuttoned, she stood and stepped out of it. She wore a corset and, to my immense frustration, white lacy panties. Garters held up white hose. If she wanted to embody the innocent, virginal bride about to be deflowered, she exuded it.

Except my wife wasn't a virgin—which I didn't care about one iota—and she was not remotely innocent, either. She was wickedly clever, with a sharp tongue to match. Even after she'd found out that I was a prince, she'd still treated me like a normal man. It both awed and confounded me.

She began to unhook the corset, but I stopped her. "Let me."

She didn't protest this time.

I slowly unhooked the garment until it slid down her torso to the floor. She stepped out of it. Now she only wore panties, stockings, and nothing else. Her nipples were erect. I cupped one of her breasts before leaning down to suck it.

"Olivier," Niamh sighed. She gripped the back of my neck. "We shouldn't."

I just laved my tongue around her nipple. After that, she didn't protest.

It was easy to slide the panel of her panties aside. Her pussy was already wet, but I wanted her soaking my hand. She shuddered as I delved within her vulva, letting the pads of my fingers dance along her. I'd moved from sucking her tits to kissing her neck. I watched her face as I pushed first one, then another, finger inside her.

"So tight," I breathed into her ear. "I can't wait to feel it wrapped around my cock."

She had to hold onto my shoulders to keep from collapsing. When I added my thumb to the nub of her clit, my fingers thrusting inside her pussy at the same time, the erotic sound of me fucking her nearly made me come in my trousers. I kissed her—hard.

Niamh began to shiver. I could feel her body tightening. She was already close to orgasm. I quickened the pace of my fingers. But it was when I added a third that she mewled like a damn kitten. Her body taut as a bowstring, she came so hard that I had to wrap an arm around her waist to keep her upright. She was muttering words I couldn't understand.

I took her to the bed, unbuttoning my trousers with shaking, wet fingers. Niamh was glassy-eyed, her legs spread, her pink pussy drenched. My cock sprang free. I crawled on top of her, and when she wrapped a hand around me, I hissed in a breath. I had to chew on the inside of my cheek to keep from coming all over her hand.

I was about to push her hand away, wanting to plunge my cock inside her, but her fingers were nimble. She gripped me, mimicking the rhythm I so desperately wanted, and I let myself succumb to the sensations.

I kissed her, thrusting my tongue into her mouth. She kept stroking my cock. I felt my own orgasm at the base of my spine.

"Sweetheart," I rasped, "I'm going to come."

She just smiled and licked my bottom lip. That sent me into the clouds. I shouted, my ejaculate covering her pretty hand. When she brought her hand to her mouth and licked it, I nearly came a second time.

I went to the bathroom and cleaned myself up. By the time I returned with a wet washcloth for Niamh, she'd already put on her pajamas, her hair in a tight ponytail, her wedding attire already put away. Had I taken that long?

I felt ridiculous giving her a washcloth when she was already dressed. I set it on the bedside table.

I could see her expression closing up. She opened her laptop, her gaze on the screen, before saying coolly, "You can go."

You can go. I stared at her. I'd just finger-fucked this woman, and now she was dismissing me like a servant?

I closed her laptop so quickly she nearly got her fingers caught in it. "What the fuck are you doing?" I demanded.

"I'm answering emails," she said.

"No, I mean, why are you acting like you didn't just come all over my fingers? *Again?*"

She blushed a little. "I just figured that you'd want to go to sleep. There's no reason for you to stay."

"You're my wife." I bit out the words.

"In name only."

A red haze covered my vision. But I knew that the angrier I got, the more she'd shut down. So I forced myself to keep my composure, no matter how difficult that feat was.

"You can act like I'm nothing to you all you want," I said, "but we both felt how you responded to my touch. How you melted against me as I rubbed your clit and sucked your nipples. You want to be my wife in name only? Fine. But I'll be dead before I let you act like you don't want me as much as I want you."

She screwed up that saucy, infuriating mouth. "You can go now."

I growled. Letting my anger overwhelm me, I took a small statue from a table and threw it. But to my immense consternation, it didn't shatter: it hit the back of a settee and bounced uselessly to the floor with a thump.

I heard a snort. I saw Niamh cover her mouth, her shoulders shaking.

"It's not funny," I said.

She was breathing weirdly now. "No, not at all funny."

Scowling, I picked up the offending statue, decided I'd take it with me for no damn reason, and stalked out of the room, slamming the door behind me.

A moment later, Niamh's laughter followed me into my bedroom.

CHAPTER TWO

Flashbulbs from cameras made me wince. I was standing with my arm around Niamh in front of the royal family's villa outside the capital, Saint Henri, a group of photographers and journalists having just arrived for a brief interview.

Niamh was barely smiling. I leaned down to whisper in her ear, "Look happy." She widened her smile until she looked demonic.

"How are you two enjoying married life?" a woman asked in French.

I replied in English, "We're getting to know each other even better now, which is why we chose to honeymoon here in Saint Henri."

Every time a royal family member vacationed here, the little seaside town's economy was boosted. Niamh and I wore clothes made from a local designer, and we were scheduled to appear at a popular seafood restaurant later that week.

"This place is beautiful," said Niamh.

The journalist kept the microphone near me, which irked me. Although the press was insatiably curious about my new American bride, they also disliked that I'd chosen an American to wed. Some of the old guard had complained that it had been a slight to choosing either from the Salasian aristocracy or from a royal family in Europe.

Apparently, there was a duchess in Luxembourg, ten years my senior, who'd very much wanted me to choose her. I'd declined, mostly because she owned ten Shih Tzus and expected to bring the pack of yappy dogs to the palace.

"And do you have any plans for this evening?" This was asked in English from a photographer nearby. He waggled his eyebrows. "You are newlyweds, after all."

Niamh blushed. I sighed internally, because I could feel the sharks starting to swarm around us. Any sign of discomfort and they'd taste blood. They'd already been upset that I'd announced our engagement without anyone knowing we'd been dating. I'd neglected to inform them that we'd never actually dated before our engagement, of course.

"What would you recommend?" This from Niamh to the photographer. "I've never been on a honeymoon, you see. I don't know what's expected."

Her sarcasm wasn't lost on the crowd. A few tittered; a few others typed onto their phones with wide eyes.

"Oh, I'm sure His Highness will be happy to show you," said the photographer. "He's had plenty of practice, we've heard."

Niamh stiffened. I wanted to punch the guy, but I just smiled tightly and said, "I think that's enough for now. We're tired from traveling. Thank you for coming."

I led Niamh back into the villa. A small estate in

comparison to the palace, the villa could still house upwards of twenty-five people comfortably. Niamh and I had taken the master suite that led to an expansive garden that was maintained year-round. In the distance, we could see the snowy peaks of the mountains, and looking eastward, we could make out the blue waters of the Mediterranean.

It was warm and balmy today, and I wiped sweat from my forehead as I collapsed into a thick chair right outside our bedroom. I put my feet up on a nearby ottoman.

Niamh sat down across from me. Her forehead was pinched. She was also gaining more freckles by the minute.

"Did you apply sunscreen?" I asked her.

"Why? Am I burning?" She looked at her shoulders and held out her arms. "I slathered myself this morning."

"No, but be careful. The sun here can be brutal for people like you."

She raised a dark eyebrow. "What, pale as ghost people? Don't worry, I'm aware of how easily I burn. The sun has never been my friend." She squinted up at the sun then back at me. "You don't burn?"

"Sometimes, but I usually just get tan."

"So lucky." She sighed. "One time I went to summer camp as a kid, and I guess I didn't apply sunscreen very well, because I ended up with handprints on my legs from where I'd missed spots. The rest of me was burned."

"Handprints?" I laughed. "How in the world did you manage that?"

She shrugged, but she was smiling again. "I'm just that talented, I guess."

Something shifted inside my chest. Although I'd been the one to issue Niamh an ultimatum regarding marriage,

I'd been stupid enough to hope she'd still *like* me afterwards. Based on how she'd refused to let me touch her after our wedding night three days prior, we weren't going to enjoy ourselves much on this faux honeymoon.

That reminded me of the photographer. "You shouldn't bait the press," I said quietly.

"I didn't bait anyone."

"You answered sarcastically. It only gives them more ammunition against you."

"If they're going to write bullshit regardless, then I don't see why it matters."

I ran my fingers through my hair. My head was starting to ache. "It matters, because your behavior reflects not only on yourself, but on the royal family. You aren't just a regular citizen now. You represent the Salasian monarchy now. When you accepted this marriage, you accepted the role and the duty that goes along with it."

I sounded like my father, and I hated it. But if Niamh had no sense of self-preservation, then guilting her was my next best method of getting her to behave. Mostly, I didn't want her to inadvertently feed herself to the wolves.

She crossed her arms. "His question was rude," she said.

"It was. But if you react to every 'gotcha' question, you'll exhaust yourself and make an enemy of the press."

"Aren't they the enemy?" She gave me an incredulous look.

My smile was lopsided. "Yes, which means keeping them close. They need us, and we need them. It's a symbiotic relationship."

"It sounds more like an abusive relationship. Or maybe a parasitic one."

"A parasitic relationship would imply that one party receives nothing in return. If we control the narrative of the press, then we benefit. It's as simple as that."

Niamh said nothing for a long moment. Her gaze seemed fixed on some far-off point. Finally, she said, "I'm never going to be the good, compliant princess. You know that. I'm not going to change myself completely."

Frustration made me short. "This isn't about changing yourself, Niamh. This is about putting forth an image, a front, where we are seen as happily in love and that this marriage is real. If you come off as antagonistic and rude, it will bring us all down. It will be a smear on the royal family. And it will make your life much, much harder."

"What I'm hearing is that it'll make *your* life harder." She stood up. "I know that your crown is all you care about, dearest husband, but you could at least attempt to act like you give two shits about me." Her voice was full of daggers before she stalked off.

I let out a frustrated breath. I had the sudden urge to get myself completely drunk, but it was only an hour past noon. The last thing I needed was the press managing to capture photos of me staggering around drunk.

During our travels across Europe, the press had left me alone for the most part. It was only here in Salasia that they followed my every move. So often I felt like a prisoner in my own country. I couldn't leave my home without at least one photographer following me, if not an entire group. I couldn't go to a restaurant and enjoy that sense of anonymity that regular citizens took for granted.

Now you're wallowing, I told myself. *You aren't going to get Niamh to like you again by complaining.*

I was considering what to do with my wife when Laurent came outside. We'd traveled to the villa with our own secretaries, who would organize our schedules. A local chef would provide our meals in-house, and a handful of servants would maintain the estate itself.

"Your Highness," said Laurent with a brief bow. "I have received confirmation for your dinner at Les Papilles on Friday at seven p.m."

I nodded, barely listening. When he remained near, I finally said, "Is there something else?"

"Yes. Well, not precisely."

"That narrows things down."

"I'm afraid I'm overstepping."

I sat up straighter. I waved a hand. "Go ahead. You've whetted my curiosity now."

Laurent smiled a little, his expression soon becoming more serious again. "If it would please Your Highness, I would be happy to speak with the princess. In regards to handling the press."

"She's already received training on that front."

"Yes," said Laurent, elongating the word, "but perhaps she could use some, ah, more training."

I considered the proposal. It couldn't hurt. At the very least, it would take some of the heat off of me. Perhaps hearing my suggestions from a neutral party like Laurent would be more effective.

"You're welcome to ask her, but it'll be her decision if she accepts," I said.

Laurent bowed. "Excellent, sir."

~

DINNER WAS AN INFORMAL AFFAIR. Despite that, we were still seated at a long table, both at the heads of it, with at least five meters of table separating us.

"You can sit next to me," I said after we'd been served our meal.

Niamh swirled her wine around in her glass. "You can sit next to me, Your Highness."

I couldn't tell if she was being sarcastic or flirtatious. Knowing Niamh, it was probably both. I picked up my plate, my silverware, and my wineglass and went to sit next to her. She raised an eyebrow.

"Yes, I'm capable of picking up my own plate," I said.

"You'll only blow my mind if you tell me you know how to wash dishes."

I leaned forward. "I can even turn on the dishwasher."

Niamh fanned herself. "Good sir, I am all aflutter."

I chuckled. I sipped my wine, enjoying the warmth in my belly and the warmth in my wife's eyes. I was tempted to kiss her or at least touch her hand. But she was a skittish creature, like an animal that was still afraid of human touch. Or, at least, *my* touch.

"What other peasant activities do you do?" She bit into a flaky croissant. "Can you do laundry?"

I grimaced. "I've never had to do my own laundry," I admitted. When Niamh was about to give a scathing reply, I added, "But I do know how. I swear."

She narrowed her eyes at me. "Okay, go on."

"I know how to cook eggs. I can make coffee." I didn't add that I had no idea how to make a good cup of coffee. "I've even used a vacuum once."

Niamh's lips twitched. "Wow, used a vacuum once. You

sound just like every guy I've dated. What is it with men and their aversion to vacuums?"

I swallowed a bite of my salad. "How very sexist of you."

"Hey, I'm just saying, guys do not like to clean. Once, I was so grossed out by my boyfriend's apartment that I legit vacuumed it myself." She wrinkled her nose. "He was so underwhelmed that when I got home, I sent him an invoice for the work I'd done."

I almost choked on my wine. "You didn't."

She just shrugged, smiling. Then she asked, "Can you drive?"

"Yes, although I do it rarely. I usually have a driver here in Salasia, and I prefer taking taxis if necessary." I thought back. "I haven't driven a car in…five years?"

"I love driving." Niamh put her chin in her hand, her gaze now far away. "They're like horses, but with engines. I always found them fascinating. When I was just ten, I made my uncle teach me how to change out a flat tire after me and my aunt were stranded for three hours with a flat in the middle of nowhere, Washington. When I got older, I started tinkering with my uncle's car, but he finally was so annoyed with all of my messing around that he bought me a junker to play on instead."

Her expression closed. "But I stopped after that. I haven't worked on a car since high school."

"Why not? If you enjoyed it so much?"

She looked uncomfortable. "I started taking automotive classes at the local career center. You could take them for high school credit. But I was always the only girl, and the boys…" She scowled. "They were assholes. They'd say gross shit to me. When I did better than them, they'd fuck around with my tools, even breaking some. They'd sabotage a car I was working on, making it so I'd spend hours upon hours just to undo their damage."

White hot rage made my fists clench. "Did you tell anyone? They should've been disciplined."

"Oh, I agree. And I did tell: my teacher, who said it was just boys having fun. I went to the principal of the career center, and although she agreed it was wrong, without proof of who had exactly done it, she couldn't help me. It was bullshit. So one day I was so fed up that I just quit. I couldn't take it anymore."

Silence fell. I wished I could find those boys and deck them. Or at the very least deck their parents. The thought of young Niamh, who loved this hobby, giving it up because she'd been harassed? It was difficult to fathom, mostly because Niamh was so stubborn and strong.

"Do you regret quitting?" I asked finally.

She sighed. "Sometimes. But I was only seventeen. It got to the point that going to that class was so stressful that I couldn't sleep. My aunt and uncle did everything they could with contacting the school. A few boys did get detention, but it only made things worse. I felt like I didn't have a choice but to give in."

I took her hand, squeezing it. "I'm sorry. I hate that you had to give up something you enjoyed."

"So do I. I've thought about starting up again, but I just haven't had time. Life, you know. Plus, college tends to take up a lot of brain space."

When she returned my hand squeeze, my rage at these

unknown teenagers faded. Instead, I felt as though I'd glimpsed a sliver of the sun in Niamh's eyes.

I lifted her hand to my mouth and kissed the back of it. She shivered.

After that, we both concentrated on just finishing our already cold entrees.

CHAPTER THREE

Two months ago

I tossed the tabloid into the nearest trash bin. "This is already a fucking disaster," I muttered, rubbing my face.

Laurent didn't react to my swearing, except to say, "Anything else I can do for you, Your Highness?"

"No, nothing. You've done everything you could."

Laurent bowed and left me to stew in my office. Once Niamh had agreed to our engagement, after a lot of arguing, swearing, and threats of castrating me, the news of our engagement became the most important topic in the palace. My parents had taken the news with a surprising level of equanimity. I'd expected them to rail against it or to demand that I find someone more suitable.

But neither of them had said those things. My mother, ever the polished royal, had merely said, "Then we have a lot of work to do, don't we?"

I'd been naive to think releasing the news of our

impromptu engagement would be simple. We'd simply write a press release, do a few interviews, take a few photos, and voila. Done.

Not so. Once the announcement had been made, Niamh and I had found ourselves in a whirlwind of press, interviews, photo engagements, and so much speculation from the tabloids that I couldn't keep up with their nonsense. One moment, Niamh was pregnant with my child (thus the fast engagement and marriage), the next, she wasn't pregnant but was blackmailing me to marry her so she could be rich.

Even with Niamh taking lessons in deportment, French, the history of Salasia, and horseback riding, along with other things every royal should know, soon after the engagement announcement, she still seemed out of place in this world and struggled with the press. My only hope was that that would change as time passed.

My head started aching just thinking about it. Despite all of the expertise of the palace's own press office, the strategy behind each interview and appearance, no one—not me, not Niamh—had been spared from the uglier side of being famous in a tiny country like Salasia.

I almost wished for some natural disaster to distract everyone. Where was an earthquake when a prince needed one?

I looked at my watch. I had two hours until our next appearance as an engaged couple. I just hoped that Niamh didn't act like my touching her made her want to vomit.

That evening, Niamh and I stood in the Sun Garden of Salasia Palace. It was famous for its roses, which my great-grandmother had planted as a young woman. It smelled heavily of roses, the air pungent; there were red roses, pink, white, yellow. There were roses so big that they almost didn't seem real. When Niamh and I had entered, she'd immediately found the biggest rose and had bent down to smell it, a large smile on her face.

Her smile had since transformed into an awkward grimace. We were walking along the garden paths with our interviewer Madame Raquel Bernard, a prominent journalist from one of Salasia's longest-running papers.

"You have to admit, your engagement was quite a surprise to us all," said Bernard. "Was that intentional?"

I glanced at Niamh. She'd barely responded to any of the questions so far, and I nudged her to answer this one. "Um, not intentional," she stuttered. "It just happened that way, I guess."

"But there were no reports of you two dating, besides a handful of social media posts of your trips to Paris and Berlin. More than one poster mentioned that you said you two were together." Mme. Bernard cocked her head to the side. "Wouldn't it have made more sense to make a statement to the press to avoid any confusion?"

"Of course, but as we all know, hindsight is twenty-twenty." I slid an arm around Niamh's shoulders. "We fell in love so quickly that I have to say that we weren't thinking about practicalities. We were rather distracted."

Mme. Bernard chuckled. If she noticed how Niamh stiffened when I put my arm around her, she didn't say anything.

"How romantic. It's like something out of a fairy tale. Mademoiselle Gallagher, did you know His Highness was a prince when you met?"

"No, he kept that detail to himself." Niamh slid me a droll look. "I had to pry it out of him."

"I suppose Americans wouldn't know about Salasian royals like ours, would they?" said Mme. Bernard.

"Oh, we don't pay much attention to anyone outside of our country."

Niamh seemed to be joking, but based on Raquel's eyebrow raise, she hadn't seen the humor in it.

The interview wrapped up quickly after that. Once one of the servants had led Mme. Bernard out of the garden, Niamh and I sat on one of the benches together. I wanted to tell her that she shouldn't make statements like that, that it wasn't helping her to be liked here in Salasia, but I was too tired right then.

I'd barely been sleeping ever since Niamh had agreed to marry me. When I did sleep, I kept having dreams where she'd disappear on our wedding day and that she'd subsequently leak the secret of my parentage as revenge.

"Everyone seems so offended that we supposedly dated without telling them," said Niamh finally. "It's so weird."

"Why is that weird?"

"I mean, don't you have a right to live at least some of your life in privacy? I can't imagine anyone expects you to announce any time you're sleeping with someone."

I snorted. "Casually dating is one thing. Dating with the intent of marriage is another beast entirely. Who I marry is important to the country itself."

"I doubt everyone who lives here is that invested in your love life."

"No, not everyone. There are people who would rather do away with the monarchy completely, of course." I sat back, gazing up at the sky streaked with clouds. "But even if some citizens are against the institution, what I do, who I marry, what I say—it matters. We are figureheads for Salasia. We represent its best interests. Privacy, individualism… those are not aspects of life I'd ever expected to have."

"You don't exactly make a great argument for marrying you."

I glanced at her. "You get to be a princess. Isn't that every girl's dream?"

Niamh rolled her eyes. "Sure, when you're seven. But I'm not a little girl obsessed with Disney movies now, and I think we can both agree this engagement between us is hardly a fairy tale."

I knew that. I'd forced her hand. I was more the villain of this tale than I was the charming prince. I hadn't saved her from the evil witch: I'd given her the poisoned apple myself.

I clenched my jaw. I'd had no choice. This was the only way to keep my birthright, to sit on the throne I was raised to rule upon.

Because if I wasn't a prince, then who was I? I was nothing and nobody. I'd be branded a bastard, and my entire family and I would be ruined by the scandal. Even if I was angry at both of my parents, I refused to let them be fed to the wolves, either.

Niamh had agreed to our engagement to protect her brother. I'd done it to protect my parents and my throne. In that, we could agree upon.

"Am I your evil stepsister, then?" I said, trying to lighten the mood.

"More like the evil stepmother." Her lips quirked

upward. "You do know what happened to those three, don't you? In the Perrault's version?"

I shook my head.

"The stepsisters ended up wearing enchanted shoes that caused them to dance to death."

"What a lovely sentiment."

She patted my thigh. "You're welcome."

ALTHOUGH I'D SPOKEN with my parents and had confirmed with them both about my true parentage, I'd avoided speaking with them further about the subject. To me, there was no reason to discuss it. I knew the truth. What more was there to say?

Niamh had left to go inside, leaving me alone in the Sun Garden. The sun was setting when I heard a rustle. Expecting Laurent, I was surprised to see my father enter.

I struggled to think of him as my father. He'd been the man I'd called father my entire life, but I couldn't honestly say he'd raised me. He'd raised me in the distanced way royalty preferred to raise their progeny, with occasional visits with nannies and tutors until I'd been old enough to hold a somewhat coherent conversation.

Strangely, I'd never wondered why I didn't look like Prince Étienne, because I looked so much like my mother. I'd always assumed I'd gotten more of her genes than his. I'd never expected to discover I hadn't inherited *any* of them.

"I spoke with your fiancée just now," said my father. He

gestured at the spot where Niamh had just been sitting. "May I?"

I was tempted to say no. But I just shrugged and said, "Yes."

My father stretched out his legs. Silver threaded through his brown hair, and he'd begun wearing a beard within the last few years. I'd surpassed him in height by the age of fifteen. He was neither handsome nor ugly, his bearing always regal. If he weren't royalty, he would've seemed almost generic in appearance.

"Mademoiselle Gallagher must be exhausted," said my father.

I was too well-bred to grunt an answer. "As are we all."

My father gazed at me, his eyes searching my expression. "Are you happy, son? I feel as though you don't seem excited with your upcoming nuptials."

I hadn't told my parents that our engagement was real in name only, that we weren't in love, and that, in fact, Niamh hated everything about me.

"Are you asking me if I want this marriage?" I countered.

"I suppose so, yes."

"I want to marry Niamh. I wouldn't have asked her otherwise."

My father's forehead crinkled. "You make it sound like it's more of a duty than something your heart desires."

I wanted to toss myself into the nearest fountain. "Duty is all we have in this life."

"It's not *all*. Yes, I realize that our choices are limited. It comes with the privilege of our roles. That doesn't mean, however, that you need to make yourself miserable for duty. You can create a happy medium of duty and desire."

"Is that what happened with you? Your own desire overruled your duty?" I said the words scathingly before my mind could stop me.

My father's expression shuttered. Before I could apologize, he said, "There are things you don't understand."

"Then enlighten me."

"Perhaps another time."

"At least, before you go, tell me this: did you know about her pregnancy before you married?"

The words fell heavily between us, like a shroud.

"Did your mother betray me? No, she did not."

"Yet she still loved another man while accepting your ring on her finger."

He didn't deny it. My father rose then, standing and gazing at the sky for a long moment. "I love your mother, no matter her faults. She was always open about her situation soon after we met. And she loves me as well, in her own way. I hope your marriage is a similar union."

He walked away. I stayed where I was until the moon rose high in the sky.

I didn't understand why my father would've wanted to marry a woman who was not only pregnant with another man's child, but who was clearly in love with him, too. It made no sense. Had he no pride? It would've been one thing if she hadn't loved my biological father, but if she were still in love with him, why marry my father? Why hadn't my biological father been suitable?

Perhaps my biological father hadn't wanted to marry my mother. Or perhaps he'd never known of my existence.

A memory came to mind: my seventh birthday. I'd received a new mare to ride, one that was such a light gray that she looked nearly white under the shining sun. I'd wanted to ride something less childish than a pony for ages, but my mother had been hesitant. Somehow, my father had convinced her otherwise.

I mounted the mare, now named Celeste, and was riding her around the paddock with glee. Laurent, ever my faithful servant, stood nearby and watched, giving encouragement when I came around the bend.

When I wanted to ride beyond the bounds of the paddock, Laurent informed me that I'd need my parents' permission.

"Then go get them," I said in my most commanding, yet childish, tone. "I'm too big to keep riding around here."

Laurent did as he was told, but when he returned, his expression was glum. "Your Highness, I'm afraid their majesties are otherwise engaged at the moment."

I pulled on Celeste's reins, stopping her canter. "What are they doing?"

"They didn't say."

I kept riding around the paddock, asking Laurent to continue calling the main house for one of my parents. When another hour, then a second, passed without any response, I was so angry that I unlocked the gate to the paddock.

"Your Highness, it isn't safe—"

I used the fence to mount Celeste, not quite tall enough to get into the saddle yet on my own. I simply kicked Celeste forward and ignored Laurent's cries and the horse trainer's commands for me to stop. They couldn't tell a prince of

Salasia what to do. They knew that, and I knew it, so I rode off into the countryside by myself.

Our countryside estate was remote, and I found myself lost quickly. There were few cars that drove these twisty, mountainous roads, many of which weren't paved. The sun had begun to set when I'd started to cry.

Celeste, well-trained horse that she was, snuffled at me when I began to cry. I patted her neck. I told myself that I was too big to cry and how embarrassing it would be if someone found the prince crying like a little baby just because he was lost.

When Celeste seemed too tired to continue, I took her to a nearby stream and sat down on a tree stump. The night was cool. I wondered if I was going to die that night. Would my parents be sad that they'd ignored me on my birthday if I died? It was morbid thought that gave my childish heart a bit of glee.

Help arrived soon after. A car pulled up, a flashlight beaming. Laurent was the one to spot me. "Your Highness!" He pulled me into his arms and hugged me. He'd never hugged me, and it had surprised me. I found myself hugging him back, holding back tears. "Are you all right?"

I sniffled and wiped my eyes. "Yeah."

"Thank the good lord. We were so worried."

Luckily for Celeste, I'd somehow managed to circle the estate without finding it, so it wasn't another long walk for her. The horse trainer led her back in the dark as the car slowly drove down the road.

When I got inside the car, I said, "Where is Father? Mother?"

"They were so worried about you, Your Highness." Laurent got in beside me. "They'll be so happy to see you."

In my young mind, I took that as a sign that they hadn't even bothered to search for me. When I met them inside the estate, I let them hug me before I'd asked for something to eat. But before my nanny came to get me, I could see that my mother's eyes were red and tearstained. She shot my father an angry glance and said something along the lines of, "He should never have gotten that horse."

This led to a harsh reply from my father. "You're his mother. What were you doing while he was out by himself?"

"It wasn't my idea to give him a horse! You never take responsibility for anything, do you?"

My father laughed, but it was a bitter sound. "My dear, let's not go there, shall we?"

My nanny came to get me before I could see the resolution of this disagreement. I could tell by my parents' faces that the fight would continue into the night. As I ate my dinner, my nanny fussing about me, I wondered why neither of my parents had wished me happy birthday.

I forced myself to return to the present. As an adult, that fight between my parents made more sense. How could my father say they loved each other when they'd acted like that? My father undermining my mother while they both ignored me on my own birthday?

Niamh and I might not have a real engagement, but at least we understood where we stood with each other. At least we wouldn't be living a lie like my parents had been for the past twenty-five years.

CHAPTER FOUR

Present Day

Whentle... When Laurent handed me a breakfast tray himself, I said, "What happened?"

"Why should anything be amiss? I'm simply serving Your Highness."

I glowered. "Either tell me what's happened or I'll throw you in the dungeon."

"I'm afraid you'll have to settle for tossing me into the wine cellar." Laurent cleared his throat then gestured at my phone. "It should be in your inbox."

He scurried off before I could open the email. When I clicked the link, it took me to a tabloid story featuring our interview yesterday.

Miss Gallagher doesn't seem to be enjoying royal life, does she? Apparently, there's no reason to smile when you're a princess married to the handsome prince! Perhaps the luxury isn't up to her usual standards. What could be explained as pre-wedding jitters seems to have become acting rather high in the instep.

The article, if you could even call it that, continued in a similar vein. My temples started throbbing. Once again, I'd been right: Niamh's sarcasm was not translating at all, and the public was not viewing her favorably. I returned to Laurent's email, and I discovered that Niamh's favorability rating was currently at an all-time low.

"You look like you just swallowed a bug," said Niamh as she entered the breakfast room. "Or maybe a few spiders." When she saw me looking at my phone screen, her expression instantly closed. "What is it now?"

I sighed. I hadn't even begun to drink my coffee. I took a sip, wondering how I'd frame this without Niamh becoming defensive.

Yet as I gazed at her and saw the dark circles under eyes, I hesitated. Did I want to ruin our honeymoon just yet? The real world could wait. Our next appearance was simply to have dinner at a local restaurant, and there wouldn't be any interview questions.

"Nothing important. I was reading a ridiculous story about…" I racked my brain. "One Direction."

Niamh sat down next to me with a plate of pastries. She definitely had a sweet tooth, and I had to admit I found it rather charming.

"One Direction? They broke up forever ago," she said.

"I meant Gary Styles. The one with the hair."

She bit her lip. "You mean *Harry* Styles?"

Was that his name? Christ, I was bungling this badly. "Yes, of course. Harry. How could I forget?"

"I distinctly remember you not knowing anything about One Direction a few months ago."

"I've evolved. I've listened to their music. It's very catchy." The listening was true; the catchiness of it was more of a lie. Their music was such sentimental trash that I'd barely gotten through two songs.

"Name another member. Just one." Niamh put her hands on her chin. "I dare you."

"Zayn Malik." I crossed my fingers under the table, hoping the name was right.

Niamh looked impressed. "You couldn't remember the name Harry, but you could remember Zayn? I'm impressed. Next you're going to tell me you're writing One Direction fanfiction."

I stared at her. "How can you write fanfiction about real people?"

"Oh, you sweet summer child." She was laughing maniacally as she began typing into her phone. "It's the Internet. Haven't you heard of rule thirty-four?"

I shook my head. I regretted going down this rabbit hole already.

"You can find any kind of porn on the Internet. Duh." Niamh cackled. "There, just sent you one. This one is an angsty Harry/Zayn fic. Also has some mpreg, if that's your cup of tea."

I began to read this fanfiction, mostly to appease Niamh, and when I realized what, precisely, the term mpreg meant, I set my phone back down. I considered myself fortunate that I'd skipped the part where Zayn gives birth to his and Harry's baby.

"You asshole," I called her in French.

"I'm going to take that as a compliment. Ooh, I should send you the diagram of how mpreg happens. It's a whole thing—"

"If you send me one more thing, I will poison your coffee tomorrow morning, and I'm certain Laurent would assist me in this endeavor."

She snorted. "Yeah, right. You need me too much to poison me." She drank down the rest of her coffee and sighed loudly. "But now you know that if you get on my bad side again, I'll just send you graphic One Direction fan art."

My wife was ruthless. Thank God I hadn't mentioned the tabloid story. I didn't want to know what horrors she'd unleash upon me for that conversation.

I PUT off talking to my wife as the day passed. During lunch, I opened my mouth to speak, but Niamh's brother Liam texted her right in that moment. Now thoroughly distracted, she wouldn't hear a word I said right that moment. That was what I told myself, even though I knew it was a flimsy excuse.

I girded my loins to bring up the dreaded topic that afternoon. After I'd had a cup of tea fortified with a splash of brandy, I inquired with Niamh's maid, Celia. Celia was a pretty thing, but she wasn't the brightest, either. She tended to swallow her tongue any time I asked her for a simple request. I would've asked any other servant, but she was the only one I could find.

"Your Highness," she squeaked, curtseying. Her hands fluttered like a neurotic butterfly.

"Do you know where my wife is?" I repeated.

Celia thought for a long moment. The question seemed genuinely to stump her. "I remember this morning that Her Highness mentioned that she would like to sit by the pool this afternoon," she said finally, "and I made certain to apply sunscreen all over her.

"She was not very happy about that, though. She complained that it was greasy and smelled, but I reminded her that sunscreen was crucial for someone as fair as Her Highness. She would burn to a crisp in this sun!"

I rubbed my temples. "Are you saying she's at the pool?"

"Oh, no, sir, she said after lunch that she didn't feel like getting into her bathing suit. She'd eaten too much, you see. She felt—" Celia leaned closer to me so her voice was a whisper, "—a little bloated." She let out a titter.

I wanted to throw myself out of the nearest window. "Is she taking a nap, then?" Perhaps if I just came up with probable places Niamh would be, Celia would finally point out which one contained her mistress.

"A nap? Madam never naps." Celia tapped her pointy little chin. "She said she'd like to take a walk in the garden. Madam loves flowers."

"So she's in the garden?" Why was I even attempting to confirm this?

Celia's eyes widened. "Of course, didn't I say that already? Oh, what a scatterbrain I am!"

"I would never describe you as such." My tone was dry. Celia, being Celia, simply beamed at the unintentional compliment.

I made my way to the gardens. Considerably smaller than the expansive grounds at the palace, the villa's gardens were special for its orchid collection. My mother had begun the tradition of adding a new orchid every time the family visited in the summer. But since my parents hadn't come here since I was fifteen, no one had brought an orchid with them in over a decade.

I hadn't brought one along. It had completely slipped my mind. Besides, the tradition was based on celebrating being together as a family, and Niamh and I were hardly family to one another.

The sweet scent of jasmine filled the air as I rounded a corner. I found Niamh crouched on the ground next to an indeterminate species of bush. When she heard me approach, she shushed me.

"You'll scare them away!" She didn't even look at me as she said the words.

I crouched down next to her, peering into the shade of the bush. "Why are we whispering?"

"Look." She pointed, and I squinted, finally seeing that there was something in the bushes. No, multiple somethings.

"Are they squirrels?" I asked.

Niamh gave me an exasperated look. "Can't you hear them? They're kittens."

I'd heard faint noises that sounded like cheeping. I shrugged. "I know little about wildlife."

"The mom must be around here somewhere. The babies are pretty fat. I got a good look at them, but they got scared and moved further into the bush." Niamh moved a branch aside. "Look how cute they are! So tiny!" She cooed at the kittens, and one mewed back.

We continued our vigil until my knees were starting to hurt. Niamh cooed more words to the kittens, sometimes wiggling her fingers, hoping the kittens would emerge. I counted three sets of eyes total. One was completely black, and all I could make out was its blue eyes.

"Niamh, I need to speak with you about something," I said finally.

She let the branch go, sighing. "I'm worried the mom will return and move them. Do you think there's some kind of trap here on the estate? I don't want them to stay outside."

I gaped at her. "They're cats. They live outside." The extent of my feline encounters had been the occasional meeting with one in a barn or digging in the trash in a city. I'd wanted a dog as a boy, but my mother was terribly allergic and had nixed the idea quickly.

"But if we leave them out here, they might not make it. And if they do, they'll keep breeding. You'll end up with an entire colony."

"There's never been an entire colony of cats living here. They'll go elsewhere."

"Doubtful. Cats have their territories and don't deviate from them. No, I'd like to catch them and at least get them to a rescue. Then they can be fostered and adopted out."

"I have no idea if such an organization exists in Salasia. Cats are outdoor animals here, as far as I'm aware."

"Well, then, I'll foster them myself."

The stubborn tilt of Niamh's chin told me that she'd made up her mind. I'd already learned that telling her "no" would result in the opposite, so I just said a prayer that the mother cat would take her babies elsewhere.

"You can ask Jacques if he can assist you. He might have an idea how to trap them," I said. Jacques was the gardener;

I doubted he trapped much wildlife, but he was the best bet Niamh had in this scheme.

"Oh, good idea." Niamh's eyes lit up. "Look, look! I think that's Mama."

I turned to see a skinny gray cat atop the fence. She'd paused, surprised to see us. Her tail flicked back and forth, and she remained in a crouch, simply staring at us.

"I think she wants us to leave," I said.

The gray cat didn't blink. It was creepy. I wondered if she was placing a hex on us, and I had to restrain myself from making the sign of the cross on my chest to ward off her feline evil.

"She looks hungry, poor thing. I'll go get them food. If there's food, she might not move them."

Despite my best efforts, I wasn't able to distract Niamh's from her cat hunting. I was rather relieved that I could continue to avoid bringing up the tabloid stories, for now. And seeing Niamh so excited, her expression soft, was so intoxicating that I nearly forgot about the shadows lurking nearby.

We'd fetched a platter of sardines, canned tuna, and a bowl of water for the cats. Niamh tossed a sardine at the mother cat, where it landed on the ground right below her. Her ears twitched, but she remained where she was.

The kittens, however, were instantly lured away from their hiding spot. I imagined their mother was completely exasperated at their idiocy. One gray striped kitten, one black, and one gray and orange kitten tumbled from the bushes.

They began to eat the fish with gusto. Although they

were all so wobbly that more than one got more food on their faces and paws than in their mouths.

"What fatties." Niamh stroked the striped kitten, but it barely registered the touch.

We'd brought a box with us to place the kittens inside, Niamh explaining that the mother cat would follow us. Based on the cat's blasé expression, I wasn't so sure. Maybe she would be pleased to give away the responsibility of these kittens to someone else.

The kittens had fallen asleep in the box by the time Niamh had gotten them situated in a little room near the kitchen that was mostly for storage. We waited for the mother cat, but she was nowhere to be seen.

"You can go, if you want," said Niamh. "You look bored."

"I'm not bored any time I'm with you." The words came out of my mouth before I could rethink them.

But when Niamh smiled, a genuine smile that I hadn't seen in ages, I couldn't regret them.

CHAPTER FIVE

Two weeks ago

I'd never thought much about my wedding day. Not to be stereotypical, but it held little appeal for the groom. Besides, I'd always known I'd have little say in who I was marrying. I'd marry some suitable royal or aristocrat, or perhaps an eligible heiress, and the palace would plan the ceremony down to the colors of the napkins at the reception.

I would just be there to say the vows and kiss the bride.

On my wedding day to Niamh, however, I found myself staring at Laurent as he repeated, "We can't find your fiancée, Your Highness."

It was so absurd, and so…expected, that I let out a loud laugh. I turned to the mirror, adjusting the sash crossing my chest. I even wore a sword at my left side. It wasn't sharpened, which was a good thing, considering Laurent looked as though he'd like to run himself through.

"She most likely wanted a bit of time alone before the ceremony." I adjusted my cuffs. "She won't run."

Niamh was many things—menace, brat, siren—but she wasn't a coward. She'd agreed to this arrangement, and she knew what would happen if she backed out.

"Sir, I'm not sure I share your certainty," said Laurent. He pulled out a handkerchief to mop his brow.

"Niamh would never run, because she hates looking weak. It would mean admitting defeat." I caught Laurent's gaze in the mirror. "I might not have known my fiancée for more than a few months, but I know that the last thing she'd ever want would be to admit defeat."

"I sincerely hope you're correct, sir."

Laurent left, leaving me alone to study my reflection. I recognized myself, of course, but there was a hardness in my expression that was new. Or perhaps it was simply from lack of sleep. Niamh hadn't exactly been welcoming my embrace since we'd gotten engaged.

Despite all of the people involved in this wedding, I felt strangely adrift. Alone. There were plenty of people just beyond my dressing room door, but most of them I hardly knew.

My attendants included mostly young boys of Salasian nobility, who would act as pages in the ceremony. I'd asked my friend from university to be my best man, but he hadn't been able to attend due to a prior appointment.

Apparently, it had something to do with "the Russian mob, a sexy blond named Natalya, and a goat." I hadn't wanted to know the details.

I looked at the clock. I had an hour until I would get inside a carriage that would take me to the royal chapel, where I would take Niamh Gallagher as my truly wedded wife.

The door to my dressing room opened. Expecting Laurent, I didn't look up until I heard a voice that was decidedly not my faithful servant.

It was Liam Gallagher, my soon-to-be brother-in-law, and an actual beast of a man who always looked like he'd punch me if I breathed incorrectly.

"Olivier," said Liam, his voice deep, his accent American with a tingle of Irish at the edges.

Since Liam had arrived in Salasia for the ceremony, he'd made a point never to address me by "Your Highness," even when custom would dictate it. Laurent had been horrified; I'd been mostly amused.

I turned to meet him and held out a hand. "Brother," I said.

Liam ignored my outstretched hand. A large man, he reminded me of an irascible bear. Around his sister, he acted like a mother bear with her cub. Get too close, and you'd get mauled.

"You aren't my brother yet, and even after this wedding, you will never be a brother of mine." Liam scowled down at me. He had a few inches of height on me. Where he was burly, hairy, and tall, I was limber, not hairy, and not abnormally tall. I considered myself the winner in that fight.

I gave him an amused look. "I am marrying your sister. Unless American custom is far removed from Salasian, that would make us brothers by the end of today."

"Quit the bullshite. I don't believe for one second that you and Niamh are in love. I see the way she acts around you." He pressed closer, using his height to intimidate me.

"She doesn't let you touch her when she thinks we aren't looking. My sister would never agree to marry some smarmy arsehole like you unless there was a damned good reason for it."

I was now almost toe-to-toe with him. "And you think that reason couldn't possibly be love?"

Liam snorted. "My sister isn't the type to fall head over heels for some rich little prick like you. She's smart. She can take care of herself. She doesn't need to attach herself to you to get what she wants in life."

"Are you suggesting your sister is, what is the term? A gold digger?"

Liam's expression darkened. "I could punch you just for saying that."

"I'm surprised you haven't yet. You've been wanting to since the moment you arrived."

Something like grudging amusement crossed Liam's face. He stepped back. "I have wanted to. I've dreamed about smashing your pretty face in until you cry and beg for forgiveness."

I raised an eyebrow. "What's stopping you?"

"My wife."

Where Liam was a bull in a china shop, his wife Mari was more like a nimble doe in a china shop. Tall, red-haired, and beautiful, she somehow managed to keep her Irish husband's temper from exploding. Liam might act like he was in charge, when everyone knew the real person in charge was his sweet, capable wife.

Liam sighed. "I want you to promise me on thing. One thing, prince. Tell me you'll take care of my sister."

I stared at him in surprise. He sounded genuinely afraid

for Niamh. I realized that, through all of his bluster, Liam truly cared for his little sister. Niamh had told me about their relationship, how he'd been like a father to her after their own father had run off and their mother had died a year later. Liam had protected Niamh, and now she was old enough that he couldn't protect her any longer.

"I won't do anything to intentionally hurt your sister." I meant it. Perhaps this marriage hadn't started in the best place, but Niamh meant more to me than I cared to admit in that moment.

Liam gazed at me. It felt like he was trying to pry apart my head, digging out my brain until he could ascertain whether I spoke the truth. He'd probably enjoy that exercise too much, I thought wryly.

A knock sounded on the door. "Your Highness, we've located your fiancée," said Laurent. He must not have seen Liam from where he stood until he opened the door further. He startled. "Monsieur Gallagher, apologies! I did not see you there."

Laurent had spoken in French, switching to English when he'd seen Liam. Liam cocked an eyebrow at me. "You lost my sister? How do you manage to lose the bride on her wedding day?"

Now I startled in surprise. Liam let out a dark chuckle. "I understand some French," he said. "Can't speak it worth a damn, though, so don't ask."

Laurent stared at me. I stared at Liam. Liam looked at us both and simply started laughing, the bastard.

"Your faces—" He guffawed. "Yeah, some people in America know French. It happens." His amusement disappeared a moment later. "Why did you think my sister was missing?"

Laurent once again looked at me for answers. I sighed inwardly. "Apparently, your sister needs some time alone, but she must not have informed anyone. It's nothing to worry about."

"You don't get to tell me when I should or shouldn't be worried about my sister." He thrust a finger in my direction. "I'll skewer you with that pencil you call a sword if you hurt her. If you make her cry once, I'll hear about it. If you break her heart, I'll run you through. You got that, prince?"

"Oh, you've been most thorough. I'm surprised you didn't mention tarring and feathering. Or perhaps you prefer drawing and quartering me?"

Liam scowled. "Castration—slowly."

Laurent was pale as a ghost by the time Liam stalked out. He finally took out his handkerchief and, like earlier, mopped his forehead.

"That man is terrifying," he said in French. "Terrifying!"

I put a hand on his shoulder. "He's all talk. Don't worry. Besides, I actually know how to use a sword: I doubt he does. I'll keep you safe."

"Oh, sir, I have no doubt. I just hope you don't get on his bad side. He might actually kill you."

I chuckled. "He'd get lost in this maze of a palace within five minutes and end up begging a footman for directions. And if I were worried about an Irishman losing his temper, I wouldn't be marrying an Irishwoman with a temper equally as bad."

～

ONCE UPON A TIME, a prince married a princess.

On my wedding day, I turned an American girl into a princess once I put my ring on her finger. She wore a gown of ivory lace, satin, and beads yet managed to outshine the beauty of the gown. Her veil fell softly along the length of her dark hair, and although her face was pale when she joined me at the altar, she never once showed that she was terrified.

The church was old, drafty, and musty. It smelled like wet dog. When Niamh arrived at my side, taking my arm, I wanted to crack a joke about the smell. But when I leaned down to whisper something in her ear, she turned away— just ever so slightly. Like she hadn't seen me come closer to her.

She clutched my arm, as if I was the only thing keeping her upright. But no one in that church could tell she was unhappy: she plastered a smile on her face, and she said her vows in a clear voice, not an ounce of hesitancy in her words.

I said my vows with my stomach in knots. I had the sudden urge to turn around and yell at the crowd that this was all a farce. I was a bastard; I wasn't the true Hereditary Prince of Salasia. I was marrying Niamh Gallagher because, in a truly bizarre twist of fate, she was one of the actual heirs to the throne.

I wanted to rip off my sash, trample it, and maybe throw my sword into one of the prayer cushions nearby. Would God strike me down, though? Was it blasphemy to destroy a prayer cushion with a ceremonial sword?

I wished I could tell Niamh what I was thinking about. I missed the camaraderie we'd established during our travels in Europe, the friendship that had blossomed. Most of all, I missed the way she felt in my arms, the way she melted when I kissed her.

I also wanted to know where she went without telling anyone. I wanted to know if she'd tried to run, despite my assurances to Liam. Had she gotten cold feet in the last moment? Had she seen herself in her wedding gown and felt only fear?

"I will," I intoned in French, repeating the words in English as I forced myself back into the present. I held Niamh's gaze the entire time. "I vow to love, honor, and cherish, until death parts us."

Niamh's lower lip trembled.

I barely remembered when we arrived at the balcony, high above the crowd, everyone yelling and waving below us. My parents, along with Niamh's family, stood with us, but it felt almost like we were the only two people alive. I held her hand and squeezed it.

We hadn't kissed in the church, but now it was expected. The crowd seemed to lean together in expectation.

I leaned down. I closed my eyes, but not before I saw Niamh close hers, too. Our kiss was searing yet impossibly brief.

By the time we parted, her cheeks were red, my trousers were too tight, and I wished I could just go somewhere private and fuck my wife until she screamed my name.

Her pupils were dilated. She was clearly thinking the same sordid thoughts. We might not be in love—we might not even like each other—but at least we had this. I told myself this as we waved at the crowd until our arms began to hurt.

CHAPTER SIX

Present day

When I found my wife outside, sunbathing next to the pool, I found myself transfixed. She was topless, and my hungry gaze lapped up the sight. I felt a little like some creepy voyeur, but my brain was short-circuiting. It wasn't capable of logic or propriety. It sure as hell wasn't capable of self-control.

Blood rushed to my cock. When I'd first seen her tits at the hotel in Paris, they'd been a glorious sight to behold. Small and pale with puffy, rosy nipples. I'd sucked on them on two occasions now. My wife squirmed and moaned when I played with her sensitive nipples.

At the moment, her skin gleamed in the sunshine, and she looked warm and supple. I had the strongest urge to go over to her and, sitting on the edge of her lounge chair, lean down and dig my fingers into her hair. Then I'd kiss her until she was begging me to touch her.

My thoughts were interrupted with the sound of Niamh noticing my presence. To my immense frustration, she squeaked and grabbed her towel, wrapping it around her chest.

"How long have you been standing there?" she demanded. Her cheeks were flushed, whether from the heat or from embarrassment, I didn't know.

I sauntered toward her. "I'm your husband. No need to be modest," I drawled.

She tilted her pointy chin up. "I don't like being stared at."

"So you've told me." I sat down and reached for her hand that held her towel closed. "But there's no reason to be shy. I've already seen your tits and even sucked them into my mouth. Let's not act like we're a bunch of chaste nuns here."

"Based on the bulge in your pants, I'm the only nun here," she said. Her eyes sparkled, though.

I took her hand and, when she didn't pull away, pressed it to my cock. "It's like this every day—for you."

Her eyes widened. She gently stroked me through my linen shorts, and I had to bite back a loud groan. "Every day? That's some major blue balls," she said.

My toes curled in my sandals. "You can say that." I gritted out the words.

Her fingers were too clever. "Poor prince. When will his torment end?"

"It can end now, if you'd like."

She considered the possibility; I could tell by the tilt of her head. But just as I thought she was going to release my cock, she pulled her hand back.

"You can always just jerk off, right? Then you won't die of blue balls." She patted my thigh and smiled.

"You're insane if you think my hand is even remotely as good as sinking into a hot, wet pussy like yours." I wrapped my hand around the back of her neck. Her breathing had increased. "And anyway, every time I do 'jerk off,' I'm imagining fucking you."

Her lashes fluttered. "Are you just saying that?"

"What do you think?"

She studied me. I could see her thinking—too much, in my estimation—and so I kissed her. I plunged my tongue into her mouth, digging my fingers into her hair. I wondered if I was being too rough, but she returned the kiss with equal enthusiasm.

Christ, I wanted to fuck her right here on this lounge chair. I didn't care that a servant could come outside and see us. At the mere thought, my excitement built. I'd never considered myself particularly kinky—I liked the usual sex, no bondage necessary. But the thought of continuing to fuck my wife as the servants watched, knowing that she was mine and no one else's?

Yeah, that made me even harder.

I pulled away. We were both panting now. Her lip gloss was smeared across her mouth, and I licked my own lips, tasting the cherry sweetness.

"Are you wet?" My words were a growl.

She whispered, "Yes."

I tugged her head back by her hair. Latching onto her throat, I sucked at the tender skin there. Niamh let out a mewl, reminding me of those damned kittens she'd rescued.

"Olivier, Olivier—" Niamh pushed against me. "Enough. We can't keep going."

"Why?" My jaw was clenched so hard it was about to shatter. "We're fucking married. You're my wife. If that isn't a good enough reason, I don't know what is."

"Because I won't survive it if we do." She said the words in a rush. Based on her expression, she was entirely serious.

Well, that was enough to bank the fires of my lust, at least. Sighing, I pulled off my t-shirt and shorts, toeing off my sandals. Then I jumped into the deep end of the pool, the cool water a welcome shock to the system.

I emerged and slicked water away from my face. "Come on," I said, beckoning. "You should at least go for a swim."

"You're naked."

I just laughed at her. "Sweetheart, you're wearing three scraps of fabric. You could be wearing full body armor and I'd still find a way to fuck you." But I held up my hands. "I'll behave myself. Promise."

She narrowed her eyes at me which, honestly, was wise. She shouldn't trust me. When it came to my wife, my self-control had been obliterated weeks ago.

She eventually sat down at the edge of the pool, her feet dangling in the water. I came to stand in between her legs, and she placed her hands on my shoulders.

"You look like a merman," she said. She gently pushed my wet hair from my forehead. "All golden and gorgeous."

Now it was my turn to be surprised. "Was that a compliment?"

"Like you don't know you're ridiculously handsome."

"*I* know that. Doesn't mean that you do." I gave her my biggest, most obnoxious smile.

"Now you're just fishing for compliments, Your Highness. It's not a good look. Pretty sure you could go anywhere in town and get as many compliments as you'd like from the locals."

"But I only want compliments from you."

Her mouth parted, surprise in her eyes. I didn't know why she was surprised. Hadn't I already shown her that I found her attractive? Was my constant erection and inability to keep my hands off her not a big enough clue?

She leaned down, and I waited for our lips to touch. But instead of a kiss, she fell forward and pushed me backward into the water. She squealed as we both went underwater. As I swam to the surface, I grabbed her, wrapping an arm around her waist. She was laughing and trying her hardest to squirm away, but I had her pinned.

"That wasn't very ladylike," I admonished. I let my hand wander to her breast. Her nipple was tight under my palm. "I think I'm going to have to get you back for that."

Niamh just grinned. "You'll have to catch me first."

Before I could react, she'd somehow slithered out of my grasp and had swum away. I dove after her. She was as fast as a minnow, and I was half-expecting to see her sprout a mermaid tail as we swam about. Each time I got close to catching her, she would escape and then splash water in my face.

My wife played dirty. Well, two could play at that.

We swam toward the deep end again. I kicked my legs, and reaching out, I tugged on the string of her bikini top tied near the nape of her neck. The scrap of fabric dropped right as Niamh surfaced.

She squealed and was trying to cover herself when I was

able to grab her again. This time, her breasts were pressed against my chest, and I watched as a pink flush crawled from her tits up to her face.

"You really don't need to cover those up," I said. I trailed my hand down her spine until it reached the edge of her bikini bottom. "Surrender or you lose the bottoms, too."

Her eyes widened. "Don't you dare."

I began to tug on one of the ties, but not enough to untie the bow. "Surrender, Niamh."

"Never."

I tugged a tiny bit harder. "You're sure about that?"

Her eyes were glassy, her nostrils flared. Despite the coolness of the water, my cock had turned as hard as iron again. I was liable to shoot off like a rocket if she so much as glanced down.

She didn't answer. I untied the bow, and she didn't protest. She just licked her bottom lip.

I had to bite back a groan. Quickly untying the other side, I felt her bikini bottom fall off. We both watched it bob and drift toward the other side of the pool.

It took all of three seconds for me to push her up against the wall of the pool. Although here I could touch the bottom of the pool, Niamh wasn't tall enough. I brought her leg up, resting it on my hip. I wished I could see her pussy, flush and open. When I stroked a finger through her folds, I could tell she was dripping—and not from the pool, either.

Her pupils were dilated. "Olivier." She tipped her head back when I lightly pinched her clit.

"You act like you don't want this, but you do. I can feel how tight you are, how close you are already."

She let out a mewl of desperation. I was all too aware of

our nudity, how easy it would be to slide my naked cock inside of her. I wanted to fill her to the brim and mark her like some wild animal.

But instead, I lifted her out of the pool and buried my face between her legs. She gasped, and I could feel her thighs gripping my head. I began to lick her clit with delicate strokes all the while I teased her tight opening. She was soon digging her fingers into my hair. When I pushed a finger inside of her, she bucked against me.

I lapped at her juices, loving the way she'd finally let down her guard for me. She urged me on, her voice raspy, her back arched toward the sky. I yanked her legs up so they rested on my shoulders.

When I thrust a second finger inside of her, fucking her as I sucked her clit, Niamh didn't last long.

"Fuck, fuck, fuck," she was saying, over and over again, and I smiled as I felt her pussy clench around my fingers.

"Come for me." I reveled in the sounds her pussy made, lewd and glorious. "Come with my fingers in your pussy, love."

She detonated. Her orgasm hit her hard, and she let out a loud, keening cry. I kept licking at her clit as she orgasmed. I also knew that there was no way she hadn't been heard by at least one person, but I sure as hell wasn't going to tell her that.

She collapsed against me, and I gathered her into my arms. Kissing the top of her head, I let myself enjoy just holding her close for a few minutes. Soon enough, she'd remember reality, and she'd stutter out some excuse to go clean up.

"Where's my bikini?" She nearly slurred the words. She sounded drunk.

"Probably stuck in the filter. Somebody will fish it out later."

She groaned. "They'll know what we've been doing."

"There are worse things for them to think, believe me."

Right then, we heard what sounded like footsteps. Niamh grabbed a nearby towel and wrapped it around herself a moment before Laurent slid open the glass door. I stayed in the water and just prayed Laurent didn't look down.

"Your Highness, tea is ready in the sun room." Laurent was studiously not looking at us.

"Thank you." I had to chew on the inside of my cheek to keep from laughing. "We'll be there shortly."

"Very good, sir."

Niamh glared at me from where she was sitting. "He heard us," she hissed.

"We are married, dearest."

"That doesn't mean I want people to hear us!"

"I'm sure it was the highlight of Laurent's day."

Niamh's mouth twitched. "Are you saying your servant has been going through a dry spell?"

"I think he's been in a dry spell for thirty years."

She giggled. But then something crossed over her features, and her giggles dissolved.

By the time I joined her for tea, she was all business. I had the uneasy feeling that she was ashamed of her giving into our mutual attraction for each other, and it gnawed at my gut for the rest of the day.

CHAPTER SEVEN

Niamh was quiet the majority of our trip back to the palace. By the time we arrived, she'd only said maybe a dozen words to me. She also kept avoiding my gaze.

Either she was upset or she was keeping something from me.

It took all of an hour before I discovered, exactly, what she was hiding from me.

"Kittens," I said, staring at the three balls of fur playing on the floor. "You brought the kittens."

Niamh tried to look guilty. "I couldn't leave them there, could I?"

The black kitten was now chewing on the tie of my left shoe. "How did my saying 'leave them be' translate to 'bring them to the palace and let them roam the kitchens'?"

"You know I don't speak French."

I growled deep in my throat, but apparently it was such a terrifying sound that the kittens immediately puffed up and one even hissed. The mother cat, who was sitting in a window a few meters away, merely gave me a look that seemed to say, *Please don't rile the children.*

"Your argument falls apart when you remember I never speak to you in French," I said wryly.

Niamh had apparently managed to smuggle the cat family from the villa without my knowing about it. I had a feeling it involved bribery, perhaps bribing Celia to keep her mouth shut. Then again, Celia seemed the type to go along with such a plan without a thought to practicalities.

"They can't stay in the kitchen. It wouldn't be sanitary." I toed the gray kitten away from my ankle. It'd already tried to climb up my trousers. "You'll need to find them another place to stay."

Niamh's expression fell. "Oh, duh. I didn't think of that. I'm sorry. I'll take care of it, though. They won't be any trouble."

The trio of kittens started running at full speed, and when one climbed on top of a cardboard box, another followed, quickly toppling the box. Its contents, full of various metal pots and pans, clattered to the floor so loudly that all four of the cats immediately scattered.

A pot rolled to rest near my feet. "Yes, not any trouble at all," I repeated skeptically.

THERE WAS little time to quibble over the cats. Niamh and I had an engagement that evening for a scholarship program for emerging young artists. The royal family had been patrons of the program since it had begun thirty years ago.

Normally, my parents would attend, but it had been decided that it would better if Niamh and I attended this year.

When I slid into the car next to Niamh, I took in her appearance: dark blue dress, off the shoulder, with small diamonds in her ears. Her hair was looped around her head in some complicated coiffure.

"You look lovely," I said. I brought her hand up to kiss it.

She took her hair. "There are so many bobby pins in my hair that I'm pretty sure I'd set off a metal detector."

"As long as you aren't hiding any explosives in there."

"It's possible," she muttered darkly.

The engagement was always held at the University of Salasia. Built in the eighteenth century, the university, although small, was renowned for its own arts program. In particular, it had produced a number of talented musicians and singers.

Niamh and I arrived and waved at the crowd before we began to climb the steps to the ballroom. Flashbulbs went off in all directions. Niamh smiled the entire time and, to my immense relief, didn't look as though she'd rather swallow nails than be there.

As the guests of honor, we were given seats near the stage that was constructed for the event. A handful of speakers, including former recipients of the scholarship, would present, and then the latest recipients would be honored. I would say a few words to open the event, and then we'd mingle and eventually go home.

Before dinner, however, there was cocktail hour. Niamh ordered a martini from a nearby waiter.

I said in her ear, "Are you sure about drinking already?"

"I'm about to puke from nerves. I need something."

"You're doing amazingly."

She shot me a grateful smile. "I'm going to snack, too. Don't worry. I won't get drunk and puke on your shoes again."

"How could I forget that?" Niamh had, in fact, vomited on my shoes when we'd been in Paris. When I'd returned to Salasia and had handed the soiled pair of footwear to Laurent, he'd looked so distraught that I'd been afraid he'd have a stroke.

The crowd flowed around us. I introduced Niamh to a number of important personages: the president of the university and his wife. The dean of the College of Arts, along with other faculty in the music, fine art, and dance departments. Even the arts minister, a member of the prime minister's counsel, was in attendance.

"Niamh, I'd like you to meet Monsieur LeFevre."

He bowed over Niamh's hand and spoke in stilted English, "It is an honor, Your Highnesses. I have so longed to meet your wife, and how enchanting she is."

Niamh dipped her chin. "Thank you so much."

The minister was probably in his sixties, his cheeks florid from most likely too much love for good wine and a belly from too much good cheese. A trombonist, he'd traded in his musical career for politics. Although he loved his wine and cheese, nothing compared to LeFevre's love of beautiful women.

"Quite a rose, she is!" LeFevre continued. "When I heard you were American, I thought, *Oh dear! She will be as round as me!*" He guffawed. "But no, you would never attract someone like His Highness looking like me."

Niamh shot me a wry look before replying to LeFevre,

"My husband tells me that you are the best person to recommend a wine and cheese pairing. What would you suggest for an uncultured American such as me?"

LeFevre gave a litany of suggestions, to the point that I found my mind wandering elsewhere. After we returned to our seats, I said to Niamh, "Excellent job with LeFevre."

"You realize we'll have to try all of the things he suggested." She held up her phone. "I made a list. He even gave suggestions on where to buy the cheeses and wine."

"You're going to end up ordering entire barrelfuls of both."

"You make it sound like that's a bad thing."

The evening went as expected: speeches, applause, speeches, applause. I had to stifle a few yawns. Niamh cocked an eyebrow at me when I finally had to cover my mouth, the yawn no longer to be kept at bay.

"From a scale of one to ten," she whispered as we clapped, "how bored are you?"

"Eleven. I'm so bored that I'd rather listen to LeFevre drone on again about his favorite brie."

By the time the event was over, we were both exhausted. Niamh had taken off her heels under the table and had surreptitiously rubbed her feet, grimacing. Despite her discomfort, she'd practically floated around the room on my arm without a word of complaint.

Right as we were about to enter the car, a photographer stepped perilously close to us both.

"Your Highness, have you spoken with your father recently?" he asked in English.

He'd clearly meant the question for Niamh. She started, and I could tell she was struggling how to respond. Connor

Gallagher wasn't exactly a favorite of either of us. As far as I knew, Niamh had had no contact with him since we'd left him in Dublin to rot.

"He didn't attend your wedding, correct? Was he unable to attend or was he simply not invited?"

Niamh had received those questions previously. Like on other occasions, she replied, "My father has been ill and was unable to make the journey to be at our wedding. I'm very grateful my brother, though, was there to walk me down the aisle." She smiled tightly.

"So you haven't spoken to your father since before the wedding?"

I looked at Niamh. I was tempted to bustle her into the car without answering the question. It was no one's damn business, and the photographer was close to overstepping.

"It's been a long night," said Niamh. Her gaze moved to me. "Yes?"

Before we could finally get into the car, though, the photographer said in a snide voice, "Then you must be unaware what your father has been saying to the press, if you haven't been in contact with him."

A trickle of ice dripped down my spine. Niamh paled, and I quickly ushered her inside the vehicle. I gave a terse goodbye to the photographer, which only seemed to make his smile wider.

Niamh didn't say a word the entire ride back to the palace. When I reached over to squeeze her hand, she gently pulled her own hand away. Her fingers were icy cold.

"The photographer most likely was baiting you," I said eventually. "Hoping you would say something that would sell more stories for his paper."

A crease formed between Niamh's brows. "Do you really believe that?"

Did I lie to console her? But Niamh was too stubborn, too capable, to want to hear lies from my mouth.

"I think we should be cautious before jumping to conclusions," I said finally.

"Oh, I agree." Her tone was dry. "We definitely shouldn't expect my dad to do the right thing."

CHAPTER EIGHT

At breakfast three days after the artist scholarship event, I nearly choked on a bite of egg when Niamh said to me, "I need to talk to my dad first."

We'd discovered through our own contacts that Connor Gallagher was, in fact, sniffing around the press. He'd hinted that he possessed information worth its weight in gold and that he was willing to sell that information for a tidy sum.

I hadn't been surprised that Niamh's father continued to be a conniving bastard. He wasn't about to keep the secret that I was a bastard to himself, not when he could profit off of it.

I'd informed Laurent and the palace press office immediately that Connor Gallagher claimed to have information that could damage the royal family. I'd been tempted to disclose what that information was, but I'd decided it was better that the fewer people who knew the truth, the better.

"You want to talk to him first," I repeated slowly. "Why?"

"Because I want to understand why he's doing this. And I want to see if I can get him to change his mind."

I opened my mouth to tell her she was wasting her time, that she was crazy, that her father was only going to betray her trust, but I bit my tongue just in time.

Niamh shot me a sad smile. "I know what you're thinking."

"Do you?"

"You think I'm a naive idiot. I'm not. I don't have some crazy idea that my dad is going to redeem himself. But he's dying: he told me that himself. Why go to the trouble, then, of selling secrets for money? He'll be dead soon. And I'm pretty sure Satan doesn't let you bring cash with you to the depths of hell to use at the commissary."

"Your father could simply be hedging his bets. It's good to be prepared, you know, in case you do need money for the commissary in hell," I said, deadpan.

"You can buy threadbare blankets and broken spoons for a thousand dollars. And you get rick-rolled twenty-four-seven."

We both laughed. Soon, though, Niamh's expression turned serious again.

"I just want to talk to him first, before the palace does. Just…let me do this."

I sighed. "I don't want you to get hurt. What if he tells you some story that you want to believe, but he ends up breaking your heart? What if he convinces you that it's all a lie?"

"My dad is clever, but he's no criminal mastermind. Besides, he seemed to have a soft spot for me, last time I saw him."

I wasn't convinced. I could just imagine Connor manipulating his daughter to believe some ridiculous story where he was the hero and we were all the villains. Never mind that he'd throw his own daughter to the wolves without a second thought.

"Are you certain you weren't imagining it?" I said the words gently.

Apparently, not gently enough. "No, I wasn't. Look, I'm not saying he deserves the Father of the Year Award. He's a deadbeat dad: I know that. He abandoned Liam and my mom, me still in the womb, and ran off without a care in the world. But I'm also worried that the palace will back him into a corner, and he'll do something even worse."

"Worse than blackmailing his own daughter?" I scoffed.

Niamh was now buttering her roll with irritated motions. "I can make him think I'm on his side. Gain his confidence. Make him think I want in on the plan."

Now I was horrified. "Are you fucking out of your mind?" The words burst from my mouth.

Niamh bristled. She was gripping her butter knife so tightly that I was half-afraid she'd launch it straight at my heart. "You don't have to be a dick about it. It's just an idea."

"You have no idea what you're playing with, Niamh. You're a part of something much bigger, more complicated, than you can even imagine. This isn't just about you and your relationship with your dad. This is about the entire royal family and what this information being leaked could mean for the palace itself."

I could see her eyes sparkling, but not in a happy way.

Sparkling, because she had flames burning inside of them now.

"I'm well aware that your precious throne is at stake here." She said the words slowly, like arrows being shot toward a target. "I'm well aware that I've married you solely to keep your secret, that if it's discovered, my brother's life will be upended when it's discovered he should be the heir. You don't have to tell me for the millionth time that I'm just a pawn in this stupid fucking game of yours!"

Her voice rose to a shout. One footman, who was standing near the entrance to the dining room, widened his eyes.

"There's no need to shout," I said coolly. "I can hear you just fine."

"You're such a prick!" She still had her butter knife in her hand. When it seemed as though she was about to throw it at me, the same footman stepped forward to intervene.

"Your Highness! Not the silver!"

Niamh froze. I froze. Then Niamh began to laugh and dropped the knife into the footman's open palm.

"My husband is a douchecanoe, but I'm not going to stab him in the heart with a butter knife." Her gaze met mine. "I'd at least use a steak knife."

I KNEW Laurent had bad news for me when I returned to my apartment, because he was bouncing on the balls of his feet. He tended to gaze at the ceiling, too.

When I'd been younger, I'd assumed he'd been afraid to see me angry. Now, though, I realized he just hated giving anyone bad news: me, my mother, even one of the servants. Once he'd been tasked with telling the staff that their holiday bonuses would be late due to a banking error, and apparently, he'd nearly bounced himself into a wall out of nervousness.

"I'm going to guess that you're not here to tell me that Salasia is going to the World Cup for the first time," I said wryly. I tossed my jacket onto the back of chair and sat down with a sigh.

Laurent bounced. "I'm afraid not, Your Highness."

I just waited.

Laurent pulled a tablet out—from where, I didn't know —and tapped across the screen a few times before handing it over. "Be advised that these images are…upsetting."

He was wrong: they weren't upsetting. They were *enraging*.

It took my brain a moment to understand what I was seeing, but when the pieces clicked into place, a tide of anger pulsed through my entire body. Topless, wearing only a bikini bottom, was my wife, lounging on a chair during our honeymoon. Despite all of the precautions and security measures that had been taken, someone had managed to take photos of my wife's naked breasts and was now making money from them.

"I thought the villa was secure," I said, my voice tight.

"It was, sir, but perhaps not secure enough. Most likely this photographer used a long lens and was physically some distance from the villa."

"And he, or she, was probably staking out the villa in the likelihood they could snap these kinds of pictures."

My hands were shaking as I returned the tablet to

Laurent. I was liable to smash it against the wall. Shame that that wouldn't stop the photos from being distributed. I knew very well that once something was uploaded online, it was nearly impossible to eliminate it entirely.

I rose and poured myself a glass of whiskey. I took a few sips to steady my breathing. "Have you informed the princess?" I said.

"Not yet, sir. I wanted to advise you of the situation first. Also, the photographer, who remains anonymous, is so far refusing any take-down notices from the palace. It's likely that we'll need to take legal action."

Which meant more publicity and, ironically, more widespread distribution of the photos. I felt sick. Suddenly the whiskey felt like a fire in my belly.

"Should I inform Her Highness?" said Laurent quietly.

"No, not yet. If this photographer," I said the word with a sneer, "loves money, we can try to buy him out without drawing attention to the photos."

Laurent didn't say the words I already knew, that it would be nearly impossible to keep this under wraps.

Instead, he merely said, "You're certain, sir?"

I laughed darkly. "Not at all. But when has that stopped me?"

And if this photographer wouldn't be cowed by the legal arm of the palace, well, I would happily run him through myself. At that thought, I couldn't help but smile a little.

CHAPTER NINE

I'd been to too many formal dinners and luncheons to count. I'd attended ones with dozens of foreign dignitaries, politicians, and other royals. I'd met people who'd been so obvious about gaining my family's favor that I'd felt slimy afterward. I'd seen prime ministers who'd not understood royal protocol, even one being so obtuse as to take my mother's hand and shake it, which was not at all the thing.

But all of those events paled in comparison to this informal family dinner my parents, my wife, and I were suffering through. Conversation was stilted, the sounds of eating and drinking filling the silences.

My father sat at the head of the table as protocol dictated, my mother to his left. I sat at his right, while Niamh sat next to me. More than once, I'd caught Niamh's gaze, wanting to apologize for the awkwardness. She'd merely wrinkled her nose at me and bit back a smile.

I couldn't help but notice that my mother seemed thinner than normal. She barely touched her food, cutting most of it into smaller and smaller pieces. My father seemed intent on his filet, his potatoes gratin, his spinach salad. He commented on the taste of the wine, but that was all.

I tried to carry the conversation, but my parents were oddly tightlipped. Niamh also tried, but even she gave up after a few attempts.

My gut twisted. Why had my father requested this dinner, only for us all to sit here like statues? I had the sudden urge to drink five more glasses of wine and get completely hammered.

After dessert, my mother said to Niamh, "Have you chosen which tiara you will wear for your coronation?"

"Oh, I have no idea. They're all so…" Niamh smiled. "Sparkly. And expensive."

I gave her a warning look. Hinting about money was a bad idea with my parents.

"I would recommend the Marquise Tiara. It isn't overly large, and I can speak from experience, it isn't very heavy," said my mother.

My father looked up from his plate. "The Marquise? No, no. That wouldn't be at all suitable. No princess has worn that dingy thing in generations."

"I had no idea you had such strong opinions about tiaras," I said.

"I have strong opinions about coronations." My father turned his attention to Niamh. "Let me recommend the Rose Tiara. Olivier's mother wore it, and my mother before her."

Niamh looked a little green at the edges. "Is that the one with the big ruby?"

"The very one."

"Oh, it's a lovely piece, but I think it might break my

neck. It's very heavy and probably too big for my head." Niamh chuckled.

I considered the wine in my glass. "Isn't the Rose the one that Prince Henri gave to Princess Therese when she discovered that he had a mistress? An apology tiara, if you will."

The silence was like a heavy cloak. My father's nostrils were flared; my mother was staring down at her plate. Under the table, Niamh dug her heel into my foot, and I had to restrain a yelp.

"Is that really the story?" said Niamh, her tone light. "Maybe Prince Henri had it changed so he'd seem cool. Maybe he was madly in love with his wife."

"That's the story that's always been told," I replied.

"Or maybe he flirted, but he didn't touch." Niamh shrugged. "Or maybe the princess was just very jealous and didn't like her husband to look at any woman."

"Seems a bit extreme, getting so upset that your husband has to buy you a tiara like that to atone."

Niamh looked to my father. "What do you think? Was the story true, or was the real story a lot more boring?"

My father looked almost stunned that Niamh had spoken to him. Even funnier, she hadn't addressed him as "sir." At a dinner like this, with servants attending, Niamh should've addressed him as such. But my wife was hardly known for following the rules.

"I don't know. I can't say I've researched the subject much. I'm sure there's documentation, letters—"

Silence. I was half-tempted to stab myself in the eye from the tension.

"There were no letters." My mother said the words

softly. "I've looked. Apparently, Princess Therese asked her daughter to burn most of her letters. No one knows why, but most likely, they weren't meant for the public to read."

"Then perhaps she was the one who was having an affair?" said my father.

"Or perhaps it will remain a mystery," I said.

"Maybe the letters were super smutty," said Niamh with a winsome smile. "Maybe Prince Henri liked to write dirty letters, so the princess definitely didn't want those leaked. Maybe he wrote letters like James Joyce did."

I choked on my wine. Niamh reached over to pat me between my shoulders.

My parents looked confused. "James Joyce? The Irish author?" said my mother tentatively.

"The very one." Niamh leaned forward conspiratorially. "He was totally obsessed with his wife and wrote some crazy letters to her. Sexual letters." Niamh's eyebrows waggled.

Now it was my turn to step on my spouse's foot. "I doubt my parents are interested in some dead author's letters."

"Not if they read them."

I gave her a warning look, but she just laughed lightly. She waved a hand.

"Fine, fine, I'll stop talking about it. But be sure to look them up some time. They're very enlightening. Lots of 'lecherous lips' and 'dirty backsides.'"

"They sound…intriguing." My mother patted her mouth with her napkin. "Let's go to the drawing room for some tea and coffee, yes?"

No one disagreed. I whispered in Niamh's ear before we left the dining room, "Behave."

She batted her eyelashes. "I didn't even mention all of the fart stuff! So much fart stuff, Olivier!"

I pinched her own dirty backside. She just stuck out her tongue at me.

In the drawing room, my mother soon cornered me. Niamh was sitting with my father, regaling him with probably some lurid tale. I just hoped she didn't get out her phone and begin a dramatic reading of one of those damn letters. I'd read a few of them, and they weren't the type of thing you could forget reading about, that was for sure.

My mother seemed tense. Her lips were thin as she drank her tea. I awaited her scolding, which I knew I deserved.

Instead, she eventually asked, "The servants are talking, my dear. That you two have yet to consummate the marriage."

If this was my punishment, well, it was a just one. "We prefer to have sex in closets. Under the stairs. Places the servants don't expect us to have sex," I quipped.

"Be serious. You know very well that if that were true, the gossip would be just rampant."

"I don't see why this is even a discussion."

My mother set her tea aside, only half drunk. "Olivier, you arrive home. Then suddenly this girl arrives, and you're just as soon engaged. You wouldn't hear of anyone asking questions or wondering if this was something you really wanted."

"I wanted it."

"And then, you began asking your own questions…" She clasped her hands together, staring at the wedding ring on her finger. "I understand why you're angry."

My knuckles whitened. "I'm not angry."

"Try not to break that cup, will you, dear?"

I set my cup down with a clack. "Your life, your decisions, they're your own, but you should've told me. Did you really think my parentage would stay a secret forever?"

"I hoped that it would. For everyone's sake."

I stared at her, appalled. "Didn't I have a right to know?"

"What did it matter? Your father—Étienne—was the man who'd been your father since the beginning. Isn't that what matters?"

"Don't be obtuse, Mother. It isn't becoming."

She flinched, but she rallied quickly. "I don't want you to make the same mistake that I did, sacrificing yourself in the name of duty. Despite what you might believe, I want you to be happy."

I gazed at Niamh, her hands moving as she spoke animatedly, my father looking overwhelmed.

"I didn't marry her because of duty," was all I said before rising to go to my wife.

CHAPTER TEN

I didn't have time to wallow in my frustration with my parents for long. After the arduous dinner was finally over, it took all of five minutes for Niamh to come bursting into my room without even a knock.

I was in the process of unbuttoning my shirt when Niamh opened the door to the adjoining room. I cocked an eyebrow at her.

"Did you need something, wife?"

She didn't take the bait. "I can't find the cat or the kittens. I've looked everywhere."

Considering how large the palace was, I doubted she'd truly looked everywhere. Just thinking about where those cats could've gone gave me an instant headache.

"I'm sure they're fine," I said. "Aren't cats self-sufficient?"

"I'm just worried they got outside. What if something happens to them?"

"They were born outside. They'd probably be happier out there."

Niamh growled, frustration marring her features. "I know you don't care about the cats, but I'm not about to let them get hurt after bringing them here. Besides, it wouldn't be good if Portia moved them somewhere where they aren't wanted. What if she moved them to your mother's room, for instance? I doubt she'd enjoy having a bunch of cats around."

"Who is Portia?"

Niamh rolled her eyes. "The mom cat. Keep up, will you?" She turned to get before adding in a sly voice, "Nice chest hair."

I made a point to only re-button my shirt so my chest was still exposed. Niamh, dressed in a robe and slippers, seemed like she was trying not to look at my chest as we began to search the east wing.

"You looked in your room?" I frowned. "Weren't they supposed to stay in the kitchens?"

Now Niamh was definitely not looking at me. "I might've moved them upstairs."

"*Niamh—*"

"Celia was the one who suggested it! She was afraid the kitchen staff would throw them outside."

"Which would make perfect sense."

Niamh was currently bending over to peer under her bed, her ass high in the air. I was very tempted to squeeze it, but I also didn't want to risk my limbs, either.

"Portia was staying in my dressing room with the kittens. I let them out when I could, but she must've moved the kittens somewhere else while we were at dinner."

We began our search, going through my room despite my knowing that there was no way the cats could've gotten in there. We then began to search other, unused rooms along the corridor. Most of them were locked, the drapes inside the rooms drawn. The servants would air out the rooms on occasion, but it was unlikely they would've done so in the past twenty-four hours.

"Did you name all of the cats?" I said after we'd looked through a bedroom that I'd never even been inside before.

Niamh smiled. "I gave them car names. Portia, the mom, named after Porsche, obviously. The black kitten is Enzo, for Enzo Ferrari. The gray-and-orange one is Mercedes. And the gray striped one is Tesla."

My lips twitched. "Tesla? Really?"

"Those cars are so cool! They drive themselves, Olivier."

"I'm surprised you'd want to drive an automated car. Doesn't give you, the driver, much to do."

"The technology is so cool, though, but they're so expensive." She glanced at me. "You're rich. How about you buy me one for our anniversary?"

I laughed. "I could, but we have drivers. Seems rather a waste of money."

"Not if you wanted to get on my good side."

A pair of maids passed us, curtseying and nodding. As it was past nine o'clock, most everyone else was already in bed. I'd had to beg Claudine to give me her keys for the east wing. I had keys to my room and to Niamh's, but there were so many bedrooms that it made little sense for me to have all of those keys, too.

Claudine had nearly made me sign a contract in blood that I'd return all of the keys in the morning. She'd been running the palace before I'd been born, and she wasn't at all cowed by her royal employers.

We wandered a dim hallway, the walls lined with paintings. Niamh stopped to gaze at one that was my parents.

"When was this done?" Niamh peered more closely to read the small sign next to the painting.

"When they were first married, I think." I gazed at the portrait. I'd seen it before, of course, but now I couldn't help but see that my parents seemed stiff and awkward. They were both smiling, but I could almost see my mother leaning away from my father's touch. Then again, I knew that sitting for portraits was exhausting. The last time I'd been painted, I'd nearly fallen asleep and had almost made the portrait artist toss the canvas at my head in frustration.

"Do you think she's still in love with…" Niamh gestured vaguely. "You know."

I tensed. "I have no idea."

"If she is, then that's pretty sad. That's a long time to pine for somebody. But maybe she loves your father, too, just not as much."

"Like I said, I don't know." I glanced down the hallway to see a closet door that, as I walked closer, seemed to be cracked open. I waved Niamh over. "Look, this door was left open."

Niamh pulled the door open, the hinges squealing. We both fumbled to find the light fixture. The light revealed a small, cramped closet filled with nothing out of the ordinary: a mop, vacuum, toilet paper, cleaning supplies. It was such a cramped space that Niamh and I couldn't stand shoulder to shoulder inside it.

"Wait! Do you hear that?" Niamh shushed me. "That rustling sound?"

I strained my ears. Then, faintly, I heard what sounded like a meow.

Niamh was behind me and had to press against my chest to get past me. Her breasts flush against me, she paused at the contact. At this angle, I could look down her robe to see her milky white cleavage. A flush heated her cheeks.

"Um, sorry," she whispered.

"After you."

"You're going to have to move. I'm stuck."

Considering there was a wooden shelf behind me, I could only go toward the door. I shifted to my left; Niamh, flustered, went in the same direction. I chuckled.

"Now I'm getting the impression you want to rub yourself against me. Just like a cat," I said.

She raised herself up on the balls of her feet to dig—albeit lightly—her nails into my shoulders. "And I have claws, too."

"Oh, I'm very aware of that."

She giggled and pushed past me. It was nice to see her like this: lighthearted, flirtatious. She'd been this way during our Europe trip, and I hadn't realized how much I'd missed it.

Niamh moved further into the closet, following the meows and rustling noises. Despite the narrowness of the space, it was surprisingly long. I wondered what its function would've been a century ago when the palace had been built.

"I hear them, but I can't find them." Niamh was crouching near the floor, pulling out various items from the bottom shelf. A cloud of dust followed her, and we both sneezed in quick succession.

"They wouldn't be here. It hasn't been touched in God knows how long," I pointed out. I listened more intently and just barely moved past Niamh to the opposite corner. The shelf didn't touch the wall, and there was about ten, maybe fifteen, centimeters of space there.

I crouched down. It was too dark to see, so I turned on my phone's flashlight. I could hear Niamh come up behind me.

"Look." I pointed. "There's some kind of hole in the wall, I think."

Niamh's hands were on my shoulders. She took out her own phone, turning on the light, and angled it so she could get a better view of the hole.

"Found them! Portia, you brat. You had to hide yourself here of all places?" Niamh huffed out a laugh.

I maneuvered so I could see the cats. And there they were: the mother and her three kittens, Portia looking not at all perturbed that she'd been found. The kittens were nursing busily, squeaking when one tried to steal the best nipple from its sibling.

"Do you want to move her?" I said. I didn't know how we'd manage without taking the entire shelf apart. How Portia had squeezed into such a small space and had moved her kittens, too, I didn't know. It only served to make me less inclined to have a cat as a pet. Any creature that could maneuver through space like a liquid was suspicious.

Niamh sighed. "No. I mean, I don't know how we would. But I'm worried she'll get locked inside. Someone must've forgotten to close the door completely, right?"

"Most likely. I can let the staff know that she's in here and she shouldn't be disturbed."

Portia simply watched us with heavy eyelids. She looked rather proud of herself.

AFTER ASSURING Niamh that I made sure the door was left cracked open so Portia could get out, I began to follow Niamh out of the closet. But when she reached the door, she couldn't open it.

I pulled out my keys, only to realize there was no keyhole on this side of the door. I pulled at the knob; it was locked.

"Shit," I said. "We're locked inside."

Niamh's eyes widened, then she started laughing. "Of course we are. Did you pull it closed? I didn't."

I didn't remember doing that, but perhaps I had out of habit. I sighed.

"I'll have to call Laurent, get him to rescue us."

"Won't he need a key?"

I swore again. Laurent would have to wake Claudine, find a copy of the key, and then rescue us. Claudine would not be pleased to be roused from her sleep. It was already close to midnight.

I called Laurent, who picked up on the fourth ring. After explaining, he assured me he'd acquire the key as soon as possible. But then five minutes later, he called again to say that Claudine had taken the night off and wouldn't be back until the morning.

I explained all of this to Niamh. She just bit her lip to keep herself from laughing again.

"So you're saying we're going to be stuck here for a hot minute?" she said finally, her arms crossed.

"Laurent will find a key, even if he has to forge it himself."

"Oh, I don't doubt that, although I'm not too sure about his blacksmithing skills. If all else fails, you can just break down the door, right?"

I snorted. "With what? My fists? A mop?"

"I thought big, strong men all knew how to kick in a door."

"I'd be more likely to break my foot than the door."

"Some knight in shining armor you are."

Despite my frustration at our predicament, I felt the tension leave my shoulders. I was stuck in a cramped, dusty closet with my wife, and I had no idea when we would get out. It was a fucking disaster. Yet I couldn't muster the anger.

Niamh was pink-cheeked, her robe having come untied. Her nightgown was made of pink silk, and it would take all of one simple movement to free her breasts to my gaze.

"What should we do while we're stuck in here?" She licked her lips.

"We could always dust the shelves," I quipped. I reached down and looped an arm around her waist. "It's very dirty in here, you know. For a room full of cleaning things, it's quite a mess."

"Are you trying to seduce me talking about Swiffer mops?"

"Is it working?"

She sighed. "Fuck you, Olivier." Except the words held no rancor.

I took that as a yes. I kissed her, pulling her flush against me. She wound her arms around my neck and returned the kiss with equal fervor. We had all of two meters of space to maneuver.

The logical side of my brain was reminding me that this was a dumb idea. Sex in a closet sounded fun, until you realized that you'd have a hard, wooden shelf digging into your back or that you'd be sneezing from the dust floating everywhere.

But I didn't care. I was pulling my wife's nightgown up, revealing that she wasn't wearing any panties, and I didn't care if we had to live in the closet for the rest of our lives. We'd make a house made of brooms and dust cloths and it would be the best fucking thing I'd ever had in my life.

I massaged her ass cheeks before lightly spanking one after the other. Niamh squeaked in surprise.

"That's for not wearing panties to bed," I growled.

"Maybe I did it just for you to find."

I kissed her, thrusting my tongue into her mouth. I kneaded the globes of her ass, wishing I had the space to turn her over my knee for a real spanking. She'd put me through hell the past few months. Besides, based on the way she was writhing under my hands, she'd enjoy it.

"I had no idea you were such an ass man," she said against my throat.

"I'm equal opportunity: ass, tits, legs." I lifted her right leg to rest against my hip before slicking a finger through her folds. "Pussies," I added.

Her eyelids were heavy now as I played with her pussy. She was dripping, my fingers already drenched, as I stroked her clit with light touches.

"You keep acting like you don't want me, but every time I touch you," I said, breathing hard, my cock like iron already, "you're dripping wet. Why is that?"

"If you don't know, then you're not a very smart guy."

I pushed two fingers inside of her at once for that remark. She moaned.

"We won't need to wait for a rescue with you making that much noise." I sucked on the side of her neck. "They'll wake up and call the police."

Niamh rolled her eyes, but she was still panting as I moved my fingers inside her tight sheath. "You think way too highly of yourself."

"That's why you like me."

She just pulled my head down for another kiss. Groaning, I hoisted her up so her legs were wrapped around my waist before pressing her against the locked door.

I fumbled with my trousers, Niamh laughing softly at me. She finally took pity on me and helped me with the zipper. When her fingers wrapped around the base of my cock, I was the one moaning. I pressed my forehead against the cool wood of the door.

"I think you're just as horny as I am." Niamh gave me a squeeze. "Are you going to last longer than thirty seconds, dear husband?"

I caught her gaze. Moving her hand away from my cock, I draped her legs over the inside of my elbows as I pressed my cock against her dripping pussy. I let the head stroke along the seam, playing with her.

Her cheeks were already cherry red. When I notched my cock at the entrance of her pussy, I said, "Does this seem like I'll last thirty seconds?"

"You haven't put it inside me yet. Doesn't matter."

At that, I slid to the hilt in one smooth thrust. Niamh's eyes rolled back inside her head. As for me, I had to bite the inside of my cheek to keep Niamh's prediction from coming true. My fingers were digging into the globes of her ass as I forced her to hold still.

"You know what I think?" I slowly pulled out, waited a beat, and then slowly pushed back inside. "I think you're the one who's going to detonate any second."

Niamh just shook her head furiously. "I'm not going to lose. No, no, no." The noes came out as desperate moans.

I chuckled. Although I wanted to pound into her until I emptied my balls inside her, I forced myself to keep my rhythm slow. I made myself watch as my wife tipped her head back, her eyes closed, her lips parted. I pulled her nightgown down so I could watch her tits jiggle as I fucked her.

Mostly, I drank in the glassy-eyed look of ecstasy she had on her face, a look that I'd given her.

"I think you're about to come." I held still inside of her. Her pussy muscles fluttered around the base of my cock. "You're getting tighter and tighter."

She licked her lips. Reaching down her body, she began to rub her clit. It was such an erotic sight that I nearly came right then.

"You're going to come around my cock, aren't you? I can feel you, Niamh, clenching around me." I kissed her softly. At this point, I didn't need to move; she was going to come simply with me keeping her stuffed full, her clever fingers dancing along her clit.

"You're so wet, I can feel you dripping down my balls."

Her panting increased, her rubbing getting faster. I pressed forward a millimeter further, until she could feel my pelvis against her clit.

"Oh my fucking God, I'm coming—" She squealed. "I'm coming so hard!"

I swallowed her yell with a kiss. She shuddered in my arms. The feeling of her orgasming on my cock, the way she felt in my arms, caused my own release to boil over. I groaned into her mouth as I came with seemingly endless spurts.

I collapsed against her; the door was the only thing holding us both up. We were sweaty, red-faced, and probably looked completely ridiculous. Niamh's hair was standing on end, and my own hair was probably no better. The closet smelled like sex and sweat. I licked the beads of perspiration from above Niamh's lip.

"Holy shit," she whispered. She pulled me into a hug, clutching at me. "Holy shit, Olivier."

My heart was pounding so hard I felt it in my ears. I held her close.

I didn't want to think too deeply about the feeling roiling through me. I told myself it was just amazing sex. But as Niamh rubbed my back, like I needed to be soothed, I knew that what we'd just done had changed everything.

I looked into her face, her beautiful, shining, sweaty face. Words burbled to the surface, but because I was damned coward, I said them in French. I whispered to her that she was so beautiful, amazing, she was everything I'd ever wanted without realizing I'd wanted it. Needed it. I'd needed her my entire life, I told her in whispered French.

"What are you saying?" Niamh tilted her head to the

side. "That's cheating, you know, saying shit in French to me."

"I was reciting the lyrics to the national anthem," I said.

"Wow, I had no idea sex made you so patriotic." She nipped my ear. "You're such a fucking liar."

My brain was melted, so I couldn't make up some excuse that made sense. Besides, it seemed like my English ability had melted along with my good sense. The only explanations I could come up with were in French.

A moment later, I heard the tumblers of a lock turning. Then I was falling forward, Niamh screeching like a banshee as I fell on top of her. I rolled away just before I crushed her, but then another female voice was screeching that I put my trousers on.

Christ Almighty, my trousers were down at my ankles still. I made the stupid decision of trying to stand up, but I became tangled in my own trousers, nearly falling into the embrace of Claudine, my cock free as a bird for all to see.

"Your Highness!" Laurent grabbed my arm. "Are you all right?"

Claudine was assisting Niamh to her feet. She'd already pulled her nightgown up, which was really a huge pity. I rather wanted everyone to know how amazing my wife's breasts were.

I slapped Laurent's hands away when he tried to help me pull up my trousers. "I'm fine. Yes, I'm fine!" I felt surly and stupid as I zipped myself. I belatedly realized that I'd lost one of my slippers inside the closet.

No one said anything for what felt like hours. Finally, Niamh said tentatively, "We didn't hear you unlock the door."

"You could've knocked," I added.

"Sir, you're right. I wasn't thinking. I was so worried that I wanted to unlock the door immediately." Laurent looked like he was about to burst into tears.

"If Your Highnesses are all right, I would like to return to bed." Claudine held out her hand. "My keys, sir?"

As I dug around in my pockets, I came up empty-handed. Then Niamh pulled the keys from her robe pocket with a sly smile.

"I wonder how they got in there," she mused. "They must've fallen in during all of the…exercising we were doing."

Niamh returned the keys to Claudine, who looked as though she'd cheerfully drown us both like a bag of plague-ridden rats.

"Thank you to you both." I took Niamh's arm. "Let's go to bed."

"Are we going to exercise some more?"

I pinched her, which just made her laugh with glee.

CHAPTER ELEVEN

Rain pattered against the window. It was an oddly cold, blustery day for late summer. Normally, the windows would be wide open, the palace tending toward being stuffy and hot.

The closed window made me feel confined. Or perhaps it was that I was having to have this conversation with my mother—again.

"There have been reports of rumors circulating online about my true parentage," I said as I stared out the window. "Apparently, the rumors have increased since my marriage."

My mother, sitting across from me and sipping tea, merely shrugged. "When have we not had rumors floating around about us? That's nothing new, nor nothing to worry about."

"Perhaps, but rumors have a way of becoming truth online if you're not careful."

My mother didn't seem concerned. She'd never been one for technology. She disliked computers, and found the idea of social media distasteful. Although she was hardly in her dotage, she preferred to act as though the world wide web simply didn't exist.

"Considering these rumors are fairy new," I continued, "it means that my father-in-law could very well be the one behind them. Seeding them in places online where they would gain traction."

"Goodness, you make it sound like it's a virus."

I laughed darkly. "It is, in a way." I moved away from the window to sit across from my mother. Since the dinner with her, I hadn't spoken to her. She'd stayed in her wing of the palace, while Niamh and I stayed in ours.

For the past week, I'd almost believed that Niamh and I could live in our own little bubble. That nothing could destroy the small bits of happiness we were creating together.

"My dear, you seem so tense. Have you been eating? You seem thin," my mother said.

If I'd lost weight, it was because my wife was insatiable. Nothing like a lot of hot, sweaty sex to burn calories.

"I'm fine."

My mother remained unconvinced, but she was too polite to say so.

"Look, I would like to hope that these rumors online will just disappear, but it's smarter to be ahead of the game than trying to clean up an explosion. Don't you agree?"

"Are you saying you'd like to address these rumors publicly?" My mother's face had paled.

"Not yet, but it might come to that. The palace team is doing what it can to quash the rumors as best it can, but it might very well be a losing battle. I'm saying we should be prepared for the worst, while hoping for the best."

I took a deep breath. I felt my skin grow clammy. I wished that Niamh were here to distract me. She'd make some quip, some silly joke, and my mood would lift instantly. But she was currently at her French lesson and had other lessons the rest of the day. We wouldn't see each other until dinner that evening.

"Can you tell me who my real father was? I'd rather know now than find out some other way."

My mother suddenly seemed pathetically small, hunched in her chair, her face drawn. Although she was only in her forties, she looked ten years older at that moment. I realized that she had more silver in her hair than even six months ago.

What had this revelation done to her? I'd been so caught up in my anger at her concealment that I'd barely stopped to consider what she was feeling. Although my mother had been hands-off with me, she hadn't been a bad parent. For a royal, she'd been almost loving.

"Are you certain you want to know?" she said.

I nodded.

She sighed, setting her empty cup down on the table next to her. She was gazing out the window, staring at the rain, as she began to tell the tale of my father—my real father, the one whose DNA I shared but I'd never even known existed until this year.

"His name was Gaspard Richard. I was eighteen when I met him. I'd been sheltered most of my life; I'd attended an all-girls boarding school until I graduated, so I'd had little interaction with boys. Or men." My mother smiled a little.

"Your grandfather, he wanted me to marry someone he chose."

Although my mother wasn't a royal, she was still a blue blood, with a lineage as old as the Valady line.

"That summer after I graduated from university, I met Gaspard. He was ten years older than me. Handsome, charming. I went to a club with my friends, and he was there alone. I was shy, you know. I didn't want to go to a club, as my father would disapprove. It'd always been easier to just do as he said. Besides, I preferred to stay inside with my books.

"But Gaspard, he saw me. He didn't notice my girl-friends, who were all more sociable than I was. They knew how to flirt with boys. I had no idea what I was doing. Soon enough, Gaspard and I were inseparable."

"I'm assuming Grandfather broke you two apart," I said.

My mother nodded. "When he found out we'd been dating without his approval, he was so angry. He threatened to cut me off completely. Your grandmother, she agreed with him. She said I would never be allowed to be around the family again if I chose to stay with Gaspard."

She wrung her hands, and I could see a red flush on her cheeks. "Without my parents' support, I had nowhere to go. No money, no real skills. I'd never used a credit card or opened a bank account. How would I find a job, get a flat? I would be adrift.

"Gaspard told me he'd support me. But when I found out I was pregnant, he disappeared. He left a note saying he'd moved to Greece. That convinced me that he'd only wanted a bit of fun. I'd been stupid, naive, thinking we were in love."

Her gaze was hard now. "You look just like Gaspard, you know. When you were born, I hoped you wouldn't, that you'd favor my side of the family. Of course, fate wanted to play a bit of a joke on me."

I swallowed against the lump in my throat. "Do you hate that I look like my real father?"

"Hate? If I hate anyone, I hate myself." She reached over and cupped my cheek, the touch strange yet oddly welcome. "You aren't your father, of course. You've forged your own path."

My mother went on to tell me how she'd met Prince Étienne when she was already in the early stages of her pregnancy. He'd been kind to her, and after a friendship had blossomed between them, she'd confessed that she was pregnant.

"He told me he'd marry me," she said. "He wanted to protect me. And, I think, he'd fallen in love with me. Well, you can imagine how ecstatic your grandfather was. He said yes for me, although I wanted to say yes, anyway. Étienne would take care of me and the baby."

I stared at her, trying to understand. "Why would Father agree to raise another man's baby? When he needed an heir of his own? That makes no sense."

"Love doesn't make a lot of sense, my dear. Étienne loved me. He wanted to marry me. And he persuaded me that no one need ever know you weren't truly his son."

She explained that her courtship and marriage to Étienne had been quick enough that, upon my birth, I was only six weeks early—at least as far as the public knew. In actuality, I was two weeks late.

"Why did you keep Gaspard's letters?" I said.

"Ah, those letters. When that silly clock disappeared, I wondered if someone had discovered the letters inside it." She shot me a wry glance. "But no, it was simply my silly son, who'd pawned it after he'd bet too much one night."

"I wouldn't have pawned it if I'd known."

"Of course not. You didn't know. That's another reason why I should've been honest with you."

I took her hands, staring at her wedding ring on her left hand. "Thank you for explaining," I said finally, because I didn't know what else to say.

She leaned forward and kissed my forehead. "I love you, Olivier. I hope you know that."

"I do."

I FOUND Niamh in one of the gardens with the quartet of cats. After our *encounter* in the closet, Portia had returned to Niamh's bedroom, one kitten at a time, as if she'd decided the hole in the wall was no longer up to her standards. Niamh had neglected to mention at the time that she'd used more than one can of tuna to lure Portia back into her clutches.

That had been two weeks ago. The kittens hopped and ran around the garden as Portia watched attentively. They were mostly squeaks and fur at the moment. When one tried to pounce on my foot and began to gnaw on my shoelace, I picked it up. It squealed in annoyance.

"How can something so small be so loud?" The kitten mewed and began to gnaw on my finger. I winced; those tiny teeth were sharp.

Niamh smiled. "Have you never been around babies? They're loud as hell, human and cat."

I set the kitten down, and it tottered back to its siblings. They began to play or attack each other. I didn't know enough about cats to know the difference.

"I've never even held a baby," I said, shrugging.

"You mean people don't hold out their babies to you to get an adorable photo? I don't believe it."

I sat on the stone bench next to Niamh. "That's not really a done thing here."

"Probably smart. It's kind of weird handing over your kid to some politician or celebrity that you've never even met." She eyed me closely. "You look depressed. Who did you sentence to be drawn and quartered?"

"Capital punishment was outlawed in Salasia almost a century ago."

"Cool story, but not what I asked."

Niamh just waited. I rolled my eyes, which was something my mother hated but I'd found myself doing after marrying Niamh. Next I was going to find myself walking around with kittens in my pockets and doing dramatic readings of romance novel sex scenes. She'd already regaled me on three different occasions.

"I found out who my real father is," I said.

"Well, shit. No wonder you look like somebody died. How do you feel? And more importantly, who was he?"

How did I feel? The question annoyed me. It didn't matter how I felt. What mattered was that no one else found out about Gaspard. I had no say in what had happened, no say in my genetics. What was the point of wallowing in something I couldn't control or change?

I told Niamh the little bit of information my mother had given me. She listened attentively, not even noticing when one of the kittens began to pounce on her feet.

"So he's probably still alive?" asked Niamh.

"I don't know." *And I don't really care.*

Niamh could hear the unspoken words. "Look, I'm not going to tell you that you need to find him. That's your choice. But maybe there's another side to the story."

I thought of her own father. "Or the story is actually true."

She shrugged a shoulder. "I don't regret finding my da. Is he a jerkface? Yeah. I wish he weren't. I wish he'd had some plausible reason for why he'd abandoned his family, that he'd gotten lost at sea and had lived on a deserted island all this time, with only a volleyball as a friend."

"A volleyball?"

"Um, *Castaway?* Tom Hanks and Wilson the volley-ball?" She sighed. "Have you ever watched a movie, Olivier?"

"That technology has yet to reach Salasia," I said wryly.

"I guess I'm just saying I kind of know how you feel, in having a dad you don't know. Is it worth finding out the truth if it hurts?" She put her palms up. "That's what you have to decide."

"Finding my biological father, meeting him…" I shook my head. "It would make all of this too real. Besides, keeping that kind of thing from reaching the public would be difficult. Too many people could leak it."

I'd been speaking in a low voice the entire time. It was unlikely we'd be overheard in this enclosed corner of the garden, and few of the staff could understand more than rudimentary English. But it didn't mean I should be reckless, either.

Niamh's mouth had tightened, but then the tension melted away. I could tell the wheels were turning inside her head, and I longed for her to tell me what she was thinking. Then again, I might regret asking. *Is it worth finding out the truth if it hurts?*

"What are you thinking?" I asked. When she hesitated, I said, "Please."

She cocked an eyebrow. "Please? Well, how could I resist?" She reached down and picked up the black kitten. Stroking its fur, she said, "Every time you talk about keeping your secret, it reminds me that you married me solely for that reason. And then I want to punch you in the face, even as my heart hurts because you've told me something that hurts *you*. It's confusing and annoying."

The kitten was purring like a little engine, its eyes closed in pure bliss. I traced a finger down its silky head, marveling at how soft it was.

"It wasn't just about the throne. It was about…" I struggled to find the words. "My family. This legacy. And yes, it was about holding onto what I'd believed was my birthright."

"I can understand being loyal to family, at least. I'd do anything for my brother Liam, and for my nieces. Even marry an arrogant, too-rich prince and have torrid sex with him in a cleaning closet."

"The torrid sex in a closet was never expected but certainly appreciated." I reached out and squeezed Niamh's hand. "Do you miss them?"

"Every day. I miss being able to take my nieces to the

park or telling my brother to shut up because he keeps lecturing me. I miss my aunt and uncle. I even miss Washington State and the US. I'd probably cry going into a Walmart at this point."

"I would also cry going into a Walmart," I said, deadpan.

"Someday I'll take you to Dick's in Seattle and get you a burger and fries that'll change your life."

"I'd like that."

I leaned forward and kissed her. The kiss deepened, desire blooming, but then there was a squeaking noise from the kitten on Niamh's lap. Before I could lean back, it sunk its claws into my inner thigh and began to climb perilously close to my cock and balls.

I let out a loud shout that scared the kitten into digging its claws even more into my thigh. Niamh was laughing, trying to unhook the kitten, but only making it hold on harder.

"For the love of—get it off of me!" I said.

"I'm trying, stop moving, you dope!" She finally caught hold of the kitten and placed it on the ground, Portia taking it by the scruff to inspect it.

My thigh was stinging, and I half-expected to have blood dripping down my trousers. Niamh leaned forward to inspect the damage, which put her mouth where the kitten had just been.

And because I was human, my body reacted accordingly.

"Mercedes didn't tear your pants, at least." When she looked up, she was smiling in wry amusement. "Are you getting a boner, husband? I'm trying to check your *wound*, you pervert."

"I'm aware," I groused.

She patted my thigh, making me wince. But when she said, "I'll make it up to you tonight," I forgot all about kittens, claws, and complicated marriages.

CHAPTER TWELVE

I waved a hand in front of Niamh's face. "Are your eyes really closed?"

"Yes! I swear they're closed."

I took her hand, leading her forward, anticipation making me nearly giddy. I'd been racking my brain to think of something that would make Niamh happy. Although she seemed happier than when we'd first married, I could still see that she missed her family, her friends, her country.

"Okay, a few more steps," I said.

"Why do I smell motor oil?"

I nearly huffed in exasperation. Leave it to my wife to ruin her own surprise.

"Open your eyes," I said.

Niamh opened her eyes, blinking for a few moments as she took in the scene before her.

"It's a car," she said slowly.

"Very good. Now, can you tell me what kind of car it is?"

She rolled her eyes. "I bet I know more about it than you do." She took a tentative step forward. "Can I…?"

"It's yours."

Her eyes widened. "You're not seriously giving me a Bugatti. You're fucking with me. This is some prank show and Ashton Kutcher is going to pop out of the trunk—"

I pinched her lips closed. "It's not a joke. I wanted to give you a gift. You once told me how you'd loved to work on cars, but that you'd stopped. I want you to start again."

She was so shocked that she didn't even bat my hand away. She just kept making soft *oh* sounds as she stepped toward the Bugatti.

Although I was hardly an automobile expert, it was a beautiful specimen. A billionaire from Dubai had gifted it to our family a few years ago, and it had just sat in the vast garage, cared for on occasion but otherwise gathering dust. I'd made certain it was buffed and shone so brightly that it was nearly as reflective as a mirror.

I pulled out the key. "For you," I said.

Niamh took the key, her lower lip trembling now. "I can't believe you got me a car."

I had to admit, I hadn't expected her to nearly burst into tears. I felt a moment of panic. Had I screwed this up? Had I chosen something terrible?

"I didn't get it for you," I said hurriedly. "We had it sitting in the garage, so I thought someone might get some use out of it."

"You're giving me a car that belongs to the royal family? Oh my God!"

Expecting her to throw the key in my face, she instead launched herself into my arms, kissing me with a loud smack. It took me a moment to let the tension drain from my body.

I tilted her face up. "You're happy, then?"

She nodded. "So happy I could throw up."

"You already did that once. You almost ruined one of my favorite pairs of shoes."

"Ha ha, thanks for the reminder." She went to the car, just brushing her fingers along the hood. "Oh, she's a beauty. I've never seen this car in real life. There were only a dozen ever manufactured, did you know that? It has fifteen hundred horsepower. Your regular car has maybe one hundred fifty."

She could've been speaking an alien language, for all the sense she made in that moment. But as she looked over every centimeter of the car, got inside it, and revved the engine, her eyes lighting up, I felt my heart squeeze. It was somehow both joyful and painful at the same time.

I leaned through the driver's window where Niamh sat. "Let's go for a drive, then," I said.

"Right now? Are you sure?"

"I cleared my entire schedule just for this."

She laughed, a little maniacally, I had to admit. And when Niamh started driving, her movements quick and nimble with the stick shift, the sound of the car like the purr of a big cat, she looked so sexy that my trousers quickly became uncomfortably tight.

"What's the speed limit? Ninety kilometers?" Niamh looked at the dashboard.

We were currently speeding down a four-lane road, the ocean to our left, the wind whipping through the open windows. "More like seventy!" I yelled over the wind.

"Oops." She shifted gears, letting the car slow gradually. But she was soon passing another car, then another, zipping in and out of traffic like she'd been driving this car for years, not twenty minutes.

"The handling on this is amazing. God, I love it. I want to marry this fucking car," she said.

"Too late, you're already married to me."

She shot me a grin. "I'll just make her my mistress."

"You do that, and I'll take you over my knee."

"I'd love to see you try."

If we weren't currently in a moving car, I would've done just that. Niamh's hair was a wild mess about her face now, and her cheeks were bright red from excitement. I couldn't remember the last time I'd seen her this happy.

It also reminded me that she hadn't been happy during our marriage. There had been moments, perhaps, but it had taken months for her to exhibit this kind of joy.

I gritted my teeth. Torn between lust and heartache, I felt like my body and my heart were pulling each other apart.

"You look like you're going to throw up," said Niamh as we slowed to a stop at a stoplight. "Do you get car sick? Sorry, I should've asked."

"Yeah, I'm a little car sick," I lied, not remotely nauseous but figuring it was better than telling the truth. "It's fine."

"Well, tell me if you're going to puke. I'd rather not get this beauty dirty." She patted the dashboard like it was a horse.

"Like I said, I'll be fine."

We kept driving for a while longer, until Niamh admitted

that she had to "pee like a racehorse," as she put it. She finally pulled over to a cafe that overlooked the beach. It was busy with customers, most of them sitting outside to enjoy the warm weather.

Our car attracted attention immediately. Some people watched Niamh park; by the time I exited, more had realized who we were. The whispers began like a slow wave, people's eyes widening as they pointed at me. I held up a hand in a brief wave, hoping that we didn't get mobbed. Although I'd gotten used to being in the public eye long ago, sometimes it would be nice to stop at a cafe without getting mobbed.

A boy and girl approached, their parents somewhere nearby, I hoped. The girl was probably no more than five; the boy, who I assumed was her brother, was a little older. The girl stared up at me with unblinking eyes, rather like an owl. It was unsettling.

"Are you the prince?" said the boy, speaking in French. "You look like the prince."

Did I admit to who I was? Considering that people were already taking photos, I couldn't get out of this one. "I am," I replied.

The boy eyed me, his gaze narrowing. "You're dressed weird."

I was wearing jeans and a button-down shirt. I glanced down. "I'm wearing the same thing as you."

"I'm not a prince, though."

"Have you adopted some stray orphans already?" Niamh joined me, finally. "That's very Hallmark movie of you."

The boy scowled. "I'm not an orphan," he said in English.

"Not sure I believe you. Where are your parents?" Niamh put her hands on her hips. "Or are you runaways? I always wanted to run away from home, but I never had the guts to go through with it."

The boy scoffed. "That's dumb."

"Um, no, it's not. Besides, you're just a kid. You don't know about a lot of things."

My wife was about to get into an argument with an eight-year-old. I took her arm, squeezing it—gently.

"Let's not encourage kids to run away from home," I said.

"I didn't say he should run away, just that he doesn't know what he's talking about," countered Niamh.

The little girl was still staring up at us with her wide eyes. Had she blinked at all in the last five minutes? I honestly wasn't sure. I waited for her to turn her head one hundred and eighty degrees and to start hooting.

Niamh whispered in my ear, "Is that girl creeping me out or am I insane?"

"I think she's going to suck out our souls," I whispered back.

A moment later, the girl reached out and touched my hand, her fingers clammy. "There are ghosts in our attic," she said in French, to no one in particular.

Niamh backed away slowly. "Yeah, that's a nope from me. Let's get out of here."

Fortunately for us both, the duo's mother came hustling over to retrieve them, speaking in rapid French. When her eyes widened, realizing who we were, we made a hasty exit.

Niamh was laughing like a lunatic as she started the car. "Oh my God! That kid was terrifying! Why are small children so scary sometimes?"

I shuddered, making the sign of the cross, despite the fact that I hadn't attended mass since I'd been a child. "Why the hell was she talking about ghosts? Fucking ghosts!"

Niamh cackled. "That was amazing. You looked like you were about to sprint for the hills. I had no idea you were freaked out by ghosts."

"I don't believe in ghosts."

"Lies." She poked me in the arm. "You're probably wishing you had a rosary in your hand right now."

She wasn't wrong, which meant I had no reply.

My wife kept laughing the entire way back to the palace. She was laughing when we went to dinner that evening; I heard her laughing as she took a bath. She even opened the door to our adjoining chamber just to look at my face and begin cackling for the thousandth time.

"Will you *desist*?" I threw a cushion at her head.

"Prince Olivier is afraid of ghosts! Boooooooo!"

I finally just shut the door in her face. But then a moment later, I swung it back open to see her reaching for the doorknob.

"You're a menace," I said.

"But I'm a cute menace."

"Debatable." I scooped her up into my arms and carried her into my room. I then dropped her onto my bed, and she let out a squeal when she bounced.

"Don't throw me around like a sack of potatoes!"

She scrambled to a sitting position, but I climbed on top of her, preventing her escape.

"I can do what I want with you," I said. I inched her nightgown up her thigh. "Because you're my wife. Besides, I gave you a Bugatti. I own you now."

"Oh well, then I don't want the car."

I laughed at her. "Now you're the one lying. You nearly creamed your panties when you saw it."

"You think way too highly of yourself. You have absolutely no effect on my panties, sir."

I parted her thighs. She was right: I had no effect on her panties, because she was, once again, not wearing any.

"What is it with you and no panties?" I clucked my tongue. "That's not very seemly of a princess."

She parted her legs further. "Never claimed to be a good girl."

"Thank God."

I kissed her as my fingers delved between her legs. She was already slick, my fingers coated within minutes. She bucked her hips as I quickened my pace. But before she reached her peak, she somehow managed to slide from my grasp and maneuvered us so that she was on top of me.

Her pussy pressed against my pelvis, my cock aching. I reached forward to free her breasts, pinching her nipples.

"No, no," she said, breathless, "I want to do something for you."

I sat up. I kneaded her ass, pressing her harder against me. "I want to fuck you, Niamh."

She wiggled. "I can tell." She kissed me with a loud smack before crawling down my body, her busy fingers freeing my cock from my underwear. When she licked the tip, I nearly came out of skin right then and there.

"You don't have to do this." I said the words, even as I prayed that she didn't listen to me.

Instead of stopping, she merely took my cock further into her mouth, her hands working me in tandem with her lips and tongue. I tangled my fingers into her hair, which made her moan.

My hips bucked, pushing further into her throat, but she didn't stop. She merely looked up at me through her lashes and sucked the tip harder.

I felt my balls draw up. I gritted my teeth. I was about to explode inside her mouth. I couldn't remember if I'd ever enjoyed a woman sucking my cock like this. Only Niamh— my wife.

"Are you going to come?" She swirled her tongue around the tip. "Because I think you're going to come."

My toes were curling. I was going to come, but not like this. I lifted her on top of me, and I didn't need to explain what I wanted her to do. She took me inside her completely, and we both let out loud groans.

Her breasts bounced as she rode me. I had to force her to slow down, laughing a little at her enthusiasm.

"I think somebody's desperate," I said. I nipped at her bottom lip.

"Me? I'm just thinking about you here, buddy. I'm a good—" she rose up "—and loyal—" she slowly sat back down, filling herself to the hilt "—wife."

She continued that slow rhythm, grinding her pelvis against me. I played with her sensitive nipples. Her pussy fluttered around my cock. I could tell she was close and trying to keep her orgasm at bay.

I pinched her nipples harder. Niamh bit her lower lip. She was getting tighter and tighter around me.

I reached around and spread her ass cheeks. She let out a surprised breath and then began to bounce faster. When she tilted her head back, I knew she was gone. Her eyes were glassy, her breath coming in pants. When I pressed my thumb against her pucker, she squealed, her release barreling into her with all the subtlety of a thunderstorm.

I didn't know how I managed not to explode right then. But I wanted to watch her ride out her own orgasm, the way her chest was flushed red, her cheeks just as rosy. Her nipples tight buds that I couldn't help but suck inside my mouth to extend her pleasure.

"Olivier." She ran her fingers through my hair. "Did you—?"

I didn't get a chance to answer. She reached behind herself and cupped my balls then kissed me hard. I groaned, my own release finally hitting me. Her pussy drained me entirely, and it felt like my orgasm would never end. By the time I'd finished, I felt like my heart was about to explode.

Niamh was smiling impishly. She wiggled her hips a little. "I'd get up," she whispered against my mouth, "but then I'd drip everywhere."

My cock twitched at the thought. Tugging on her hair, I licked the sweat from her throat. "Where did you come from?" I found myself asking.

She didn't answer, because I didn't let her. I kissed her, plunging my tongue into her mouth, massaging her shoulders, her back, her ass. I didn't want this to end. Even when she finally dismounted, I was still half-hard.

She snuggled against me as we simply lay in contented silence.

"Was that enough to pay for the Bugatti?" Niamh asked some time later.

I just stared at her. Then I spluttered into laughter.

"Well, now I'm offended." She wrinkled her nose.

I patted her delicious ass. "Sweetheart, that just paid for an entire fleet of Bugattis."

CHAPTER THIRTEEN

It was early hours when I awoke. Rain was falling softly against the window. Yawning, I glanced at the clock: five a.m. I wouldn't need to be awake for another two hours.

I considered going back to sleep, but then Niamh opened her eyes. She stared up at me, her gaze hazy, like she wasn't sure who I was.

"*Bonjour,*" I said, brushing a few strands of hair from her forehead.

She yawned widely. "What time is it? Oh God, it's way too early to be awake." She turned over and hugged a pillow closely. "Wake me up at a reasonable hour."

"So, noon?"

"I don't sleep in that late."

"Oh, then eleven a.m."

I could hear her rolling her eyes. I slung an arm over her waist, capturing her hand in mine. I kissed her ear then blew a raspberry against her shoulder.

"Go away! You're annoying." She pushed me away,

albeit half-heartedly. Our struggle soon devolved into a wrestle match that I won within ten seconds.

My wife now pinned beneath me, I had both of her wrists in my grip. "You were saying?" I said.

"I was saying that you were *trés annoying*!" She said the word *annoying* in a French accent.

"All those French lessons and you can't remember the word for 'annoying'?"

"Apparently they banned it from being taught, because a certain prince got mad about it."

I ground my hips against her, mostly just to tease her with the idea of morning sex. I was currently torn between simply continuing to annoy her or fuck her senseless. Perhaps I could manage both simultaneously.

"I'm flattered that you think I'm so powerful that I could effectively ban a word from the French language," I said.

"Powerful or arrogant. High-handed. Overbearing. See, I can list plenty of English adjectives."

"And what husband doesn't want that in his wife?"

I could see Niamh's expression shutter. Getting off of her, I waited for her to roll next to me. But she kept space between us now, and it hurt more than I cared to admit.

"What's going to happen to us?" she said finally.

"What do you mean?"

"I mean this. This marriage. This thing we decided to do. Are we just going to keep the big secret a big secret for eternity? Stay married and act like it doesn't exist?"

"Divorce is always an option."

"And if your real father is revealed? Then you're back at square one." Niamh flipped over to face me. "So that doesn't make sense, and it'll mean Liam is roped into this."

Had I thought about the future? What our lives would become? I'd assumed we'd play our parts and then live separate lives, as most royals did eventually. But now the thought of that was almost too painful to contemplate.

"Do you want to leave?" I said the words through gritted teeth.

"No. For some insane reason, I don't." Niamh's tone lightened. "I can't take the Bugatti with me, anyway."

"Ah, so you've seen through me."

She blinked. I wondered if I'd said too much, revealed my hand too early. But then she shoved at my shoulder. "So that's why you let me have it? As a way to make me stay? No wonder you didn't get me some huge diamond necklace. Can't take a Bugatti on a plane."

Niamh went quiet, picking at a stray thread on the duvet. "What about kids? Aren't you supposed to have at least one, for that whole 'keeping the throne' thing?"

I felt like I was suddenly on thin ice. One wrong move, and I'd plunge into freezing, heart-stopping waters.

"Would you believe me if I said I hadn't thought about it?" I asked.

"No, I don't believe you."

I shrugged one shoulder. "I knew I'd have to do it someday. I had a few thoughts about how I could persuade you to bear my child, I'll admit. Beyond that, children had always seemed like something that would happen to me, not something I'd choose to have."

"That's kind of depressing."

"What about you? Do you want children?"

She kept pulling at that stray thread. Laurent would

have a conniption if he saw what she was doing to the poor duvet.

"I never honestly thought about it until my niece Fiona was born. She was the first kid I actually wanted to see photos of, you know? With anyone else's baby, it was like, 'Okay, that's nice, but it looks like a red, squishy potato.'"

"Please don't tell me you called someone's baby a red, squishy potato."

"Not to their face." She smiled. "But then when I first met Fiona, she was also a red, squishy potato, but she meant something to me, you know?"

I had to admit, I didn't know. As an only child—as far as I knew, perhaps I had dozens of siblings I'd never meet—I wouldn't have any nieces or nephews.

Niamh reached over and began scrolling through her phone. "Here's Fiona when she was born." She began to show me photos of first Fiona, and then Dahlia, her second niece. Fiona was red-haired like her mother Mari, while Dahlia looked like Liam. She even had his frown. In one photo, she was frowning while wearing a flower costume, ostensibly for Halloween. I'd never seen a young child look so cute yet so ferocious.

"I mean, I'm biased," said Niamh, "but they're pretty fucking cute. Fiona is so smart. She loves to be read to, but if you read a line wrong, she'll correct you. She's memorized all of her favorite books."

"And Dahlia?"

"Let's just say my sister-in-law has to put her on a leash to keep her from running off. Usually after somebody's dog. Or after a pigeon. She's not picky, really."

"She sounds like she'll be a menace, just like you."

Niamh grinned. "Exactly."

I kissed her forehead. Taking her hand, I admitted, "I think I can see children in my future. Maybe not any time soon, but it's more than a vague idea now."

"Yeah, I know. I feel the same."

The ice beneath my feet was cracking. I could hear it, the sound ominous, yet I found myself not feeling scared. Instead, as I kissed my wife, I found myself only excited to see what our future would bring.

WEEKS PASSED. Niamh essentially moved into my chambers, sleeping in my bed—*our* bed—every night. I attended a handful of engagements, while Niamh continued with her lessons and joined me at a few of the engagements as necessary. She much preferred to stay out of the spotlight, and as the public seemed not quite as fascinated with her as they'd been earlier in the summer, I didn't try to change her mind.

Everything seemed to be going smoothly. Our relationship was progressing; the threats of scandal that had plagued us seemed to have disappeared.

I became complacent. I became naive.

Because when you lived your entire life in the public eye, you might have a break from the spotlight. It always ends, however. The claws of gossip, of speculation, inevitably disrupted the peace—eventually.

After dinner one evening, when Niamh and I had already returned to our chamber and were discussing whether we wanted to stroll the gardens, Laurent called the phone next to my bedside.

Niamh's clothes remained in her dressing room in her chamber, and she was currently changing into something more suitable for a walk. When the phone began to ring, I had the eerie feeling that it wasn't to wish me a good night's rest.

Laurent, for once, didn't mince words. "Your Highness, forgive the intrusion. The princess's father wishes to see you."

"When?"

"Now, sir. He's here, wanting an audience."

I gripped the receiver, listening for the sound of my wife coming into my bedroom. I hoped the cats would distract her until I finished speaking with Laurent.

"He wishes to see me? Are you certain?"

"Quite. He was adamant that he speaks to you, without Her Highness knowing. He says if you don't come to speak with him, he'll, quote, 'leak every damn thing on the Internet.'"

I swore. And I swore again when I heard the creak of the adjoining door open. Laurent told me where Connor Gallagher was lying in wait the moment before Niamh came into the bedroom.

She saw my expression and frowned. "What is it?"

I forced myself to smile, although I was certain it was strained. I rose and kissed her forehead. "I have a matter that I need to attend to. I'm sorry I won't be able to take that walk with you tonight."

"What matter?" Niamh's eyes narrowed. "What aren't you telling me?"

"It's nothing." When she looked more annoyed, I added, "It's actually rather stupid. Apparently, Laurent agreed that

I'd be interviewed tomorrow, but he'd neglected to provide me with the questions."

"So you're having to prepare right now? At nine o'clock p.m.? It can probably wait until morning."

"Afraid not. The interview is early in the morning."

Niamh remained skeptical, but then one of the kittens barreled through the partially shut door and started climbing up one of the window curtains. Soon enough, the two others were copying their sibling.

"Crap, I'll get them—" Niamh hurried to the window and began plucking kittens from curtains like you'd pick apples from a tree, albeit apples with needle-sharp claws that yelled in protest.

I headed to the north entrance of the palace, where the public would normally enter when given a tour. It was generally not in use by the royal family; instead, it functioned more like a museum. I had no idea how Connor Gallagher had managed to get inside. It wasn't as though you could simply walk up the entrance and meander inside without security stopping you.

Laurent found me outside the room that contained my father-in-law. "Your Highness, I must apologize. One of the security guards contacted me about him, saying that he was Her Highness's father. He wouldn't leave until I agreed to tell you he was here. If you wish, we can have him thrown out."

"No, that isn't necessary. If he has something to say to me, he can say it." Besides, I knew that he'd make good on this threat to reveal my secret if I didn't. He held all of the power. Apparently, all of the money in the world wouldn't keep Connor Gallagher from demanding more.

"I will stand outside if you should need me, sir." Laurent stood at attention near the doorway. Not far away were two security guards, who bowed when they saw me.

Connor was lounging on a velvet settee when I entered the parlor. It was a small room, at least by the palace's standards, and I had a feeling Laurent had chosen this one because it wasn't a room that would receive guests. Connor wasn't a guest; he was an intruder.

Connor was thinner and more haggard than when I'd seen him last. Despite the new lines around his mouth and eyes, his expression remained surprisingly bland.

He didn't stand when he saw me enter. He merely sat up and laughed when I sat stiffly in a chair across from him.

"I'd get up and bow, but my bones hurt today," said Connor.

"In the grand scheme of things, it doesn't particularly matter."

"Ah, you're practical. That's uncommon in rich people like yourself. Pretty sure if your servant realized I wasn't calling you 'Your Majesty,' he'd have a stroke."

"He would, only because I'm called 'Your Highness.'"

Connor laughed. "Touché." He leaned against the back of the settee. "I think we'd be friends, in another lifetime."

"Doubtful. I don't keep friends who use their own daughter for their advantage."

He smiled, but there was no joy in it. "Then let's not waste any more of my time or yours. You have money; I want money. You give me money, or I tell everyone who you are. Pretty simple."

I had to restrain myself from punching him in the throat. He was so calm, so amused, that I saw red across my vision. Not just because he was threatening me, but because he'd use his own daughter like this. It was despicable.

"What if I told you that I don't care if you tell the world about my parentage?" I folded my hands, forcing calm into my voice. "Then what?"

"I'd say you were a bad fucking liar. You look like you're about to spew. Green about the gills, princeling. Then again, you wouldn't be a prince much longer afterward."

I wondered if Connor was all bluster. If and when he released this story, he wouldn't have any leverage over me. He'd be giving away the one card he held in his hand.

"I married your daughter, one of the heirs, for that sole reason. And if she were already pregnant…" I let the possibility dangle between us.

Niamh, of course, wasn't pregnant. I didn't know if she'd ever agree to produce an heir. But Connor didn't know that.

Connor's expression turned dark. "Then if you don't care about yourself, then maybe you'd want to keep your wife safe. There are photos, you know, photos of your wife, that could also be released."

I froze. Connor had been the one threatening to release those topless photos of Niamh. *Her own father.* I felt sick. Rage like I'd never felt surged through my veins.

In an instant, I was grabbing Connor by the shirt collar, shaking him as he tried desperately to pry my hands away.

"You would threaten your own daughter, your flesh and blood, like this?" I shook him one last time and then thrust him away from me. "You're disgusting. You don't deserve to even kiss Niamh's feet."

Connor was coughing, his face still blue. I heard furious

knocking in the door and Laurent's voice, "Are you all right, Your Highness? Sir!"

I quickly assured Laurent I was fine before locking the door in his distressed face. Returning to Connor, I waited for him to catch his breath. The only reason I didn't kill him right then and there was because poor Laurent didn't deserve to have to clean up Connor's cowardly, vile remains.

"You surprise me," said Connor, his voice hoarse. "Didn't expect a pretty rich boy like yourself to have such fight in him."

"We're both full of surprises tonight," I said scathingly.

"You must really care about my daughter? I didn't think you would. Thought you were more like me. Couldn't blame you if you were. Everybody has to get what they're due in this world. I want money; you want your throne. It just so happens that Niamh is the key to both of us getting those things."

I stilled, torn between beating this man into a pulp or throwing him out of a window. Mostly, I hated that he'd dared to compare us, as if I were on his level.

I might've forced Niamh's hand; I might've created this situation. But was I just like Connor Gallagher, truly only caring about myself, no matter who got hurt?

Connor chuckled. "Hit a mark? Don't despair, dearest son-in-law. There are worse fates than having ambition."

"Ambition is one thing—destroying your own daughter's reputation for it is another. Don't act as though we're similar people."

Connor shrugged. "I didn't come here to chitchat. I came here for my money." He leaned forward, resolve in his hardened face. "Either you pay up or everything gets released. The photos, the story. All of it. Your life, Niamh's, and your parents' lives come crashing down. All you have to do is a write me a check for ten million Euro. A small price to pay, yes?"

"You're insane."

I turned to go, no longer interested in bargaining with the devil. I'd pay him ten million Euro, and then he'd ask for twenty million more.

"You have two weeks," said Connor at my retreating figure. "Two weeks, or I pull the trigger."

I didn't even look at him as I replied, "Security will escort you out. If you show your face here again, I'll have you arrested for trespassing."

CHAPTER FOURTEEN

The press office in the palace was moving faster than I'd ever seen it. Along with the coterie of lawyers the palace had on hand, everyone was working tirelessly to stop Connor Gallagher from making good on his threats.

Despite his threats, there wasn't enough to arrest him, considering he didn't threaten my life or anyone else's. Threatening to release information, or photos that we had no proof he'd taken, wasn't enough for the police. And he hadn't trespassed on palace grounds when he'd been admitted after demanding to see me.

And where was Connor Gallagher, while not lurking about the palace? No one knew. He was a slippery figure, to say the least. We had private detectives searching Saint Henri, trying to find anyone who'd seen an Irishman of middling height and build. It wasn't as though there were masses of Irishman here in Salasia. He should stick out like a sore thumb.

Yet as far as I knew, Connor was smart enough to lay low for the next two weeks.

"Can't we just have someone kill him?" I said, only half-jokingly, to Laurent a few mornings after my conversation with Connor.

Laurent didn't bat an eyelash. "Unfortunately, the monarchy hasn't been able to execute criminals in over a century."

"Shame. Niamh's idea about guillotines wasn't entirely insane, now that I think of it."

Of course, I had no interest in killing my father-in-law. This wasn't some spy novel; this was an old man, presumably one who was dying, who wanted to die with enough money that he'd never have to worry about his bills being paid again.

"What's the point of wanting ten million if you're dying?" I'd wondered aloud to Laurent earlier. "No amount of money is going to keep death from knocking."

"Perhaps there is no reason beyond wanting to prove a point. That he can make the monarchy that had hurt his mother bend to his will," Laurent had replied.

It made sense. Princess Mary, Connor's mother, had been disowned by the family when she'd married Sean Gallagher. The story had been such a stain on the royal family that I'd never heard of it until I'd had the misfortune of meeting Connor Gallagher.

Then again, I wouldn't have met Niamh, either. Could I really regret everything that had happened since then? That my life had been completely upended beyond anything I could've imagined?

I might've said yes before I'd married Niamh. Now, I didn't think I could.

After receiving an update on the legal and PR teams'

progress, I returned to the east wing, where Niamh was currently having lessons. She'd been suspicious ever since I'd had the meeting with her father. I'd wanted to tell her everything, and it had taken everything inside me not to spill the entire story to her.

But the other part of me wanted to take care of this myself. I didn't want her to worry. I'd created this mess by involving her; I'd fix it without causing her more stress. I wanted to protect her from this world I'd forced her to join, even if she might be angry with me later when, or even if, she discovered the truth.

Celia, Niamh's maid, approached me with a worried expression. "Oh, Your Highness, the cats—" She sighed deeply. "They are not staying here forever, yes?"

"Have they gotten into something else?"

"Oh, they are so naughty! They have chewed on purses, shoes, even climbed up some of Her Highness's gowns! They are terrors yet madam does not seem to think so!"

"Then perhaps we need to create a space just for them," I mused. "A cat room. Can you ask Claudine about putting that together?"

"If that means I can get them out of madam's dressing room, of course. I will put it together myself if I have to!"

Celia hurried off, talking to herself under her breath about devil cats that would dare to ruin expensive purses and gowns.

I didn't blame her for her frustration; her job was to care for Niamh and Niamh's things. Having a trio of kittens making your job harder, despite how cute they were, would be immensely frustrating.

A week later, Claudine, Celia, and a number of other

servants created a cat room that seemed straight out of a fairy tale: cat trees that looked like actual trees, perches that were shaped like toadstools, and beds that were shaped like flowers. There were more toys than any four cats could ever play with, along with wall paths that meant the cats could get as high as their feline hearts desired.

And very conveniently, the room was right next door to Niamh's chambers, so she didn't have to go far for feline company.

"Did you put this together?" Niamh whirled on me.

"I can't take the credit. Celia was behind it, along with Claudine. I believe the motivation was more to remove the cats from your dressing room than pleasing the cats themselves."

Niamh laughed. "Poor Celia. I had no idea she was that desperate to get the cats out of my room." Niamh crouched down where Enzo and Tesla were currently wrestling. Tesla kicked Enzo in the face, which made Enzo yowl in protest.

"You might not take any credit, but you did come around to liking the cats." Niamh rose and smiled at me. "Admit it: they're cute."

At the moment, Mercedes was trying to get onto my shoulder from a nearby cat tree, her claws sinking into my skin. "I admit nothing."

"You love them. You can't bear to be parted from them." Niamh flung her arms around me. "You've become a cat person. Admit it."

Mercedes finally jumped onto my shoulder. I winced as her claws dug in farther. Petting her, I replied, "I'm a cat person if it means making you smile."

Niamh's smile widened. I would've kissed her, but then

we'd have a kitten falling onto my wife's face, which I didn't think either would've appreciated. Instead, Niamh stood on her tiptoes and kissed me.

"Thank you. This is amazing." She gave me one last loud smacking kiss. "We'll fill this entire palace with cats in no time."

"Four is plenty."

"We could easily take on four more. Another litter. We could even foster some cats, too."

I placed Mercedes on a nearby perch and took Niamh's hands. "No. More. Cats."

"How can you put a limit on how many cats you have?"

"Easy. Four is my limit. The end."

She waved a hand. "You say that now," she said breezily. She went to a window, where Celia had made certain a bird feeder was hung nearby. Two sparrows were eating at the feeder while Portia watched with a rapidly thumping tail. I wondered if the sparrows had any idea how close to death they were, that only a pane of glass was keeping them safe right then.

Niamh scratched Portia behind her ears before beckoning me over. She wouldn't look me in the eye, and she seemed suddenly nervous.

"You keep giving me all of these things," she began. "The car, now the cat room."

"The cat room was more for Celia, if I were being honest."

"That being said, you've been showing me in a lot of ways that you care about me." Niamh looked up at me through her lashes. "At least, I think you care. You could just be bribing me to keep me happy."

I didn't know how to reply to that. Luckily, Niamh kept talking.

"Everything that's happened, us together, the gestures…"

She was now petting Portia to the point that Portia's ears were going back in annoyance. When Niamh didn't take the hint, Portia gave her a light smack and then hopped onto a platform above our heads with as much of a huff as a cat could give off.

"Um, yeah. What was I saying?"

I said gently, "With everything that's happened…"

"Yes, I mean, with everything that's happened. I just was thinking…" Niamh took in a deep breath. Then exhaled. Finally, she blurted, "I think I'm in love with you."

The only sounds were the sounds of the kittens playing, along with Portia's tail lightly hitting the windowpane above us. Most of all, I could hear my heart pounding in my ears.

"Niamh," I said. "Look at me."

She slowly turned her gaze up toward mine.

"I'm in love with you, too."

And then before she could start babbling, I kissed her. She laughed, a joyous sound, a sound that sent me into a tailspin of joy. I hadn't realized that I loved her until she said the words aloud. Now, though, it was like everything had suddenly clicked into place.

"Oh, thank God," said Niamh, panting a little. "I wasn't sure you felt the same."

"I didn't know until this moment."

"Well, I'll try to take that as a compliment, I guess."

I pinched her chin gently. "It is a compliment. I'm a prince, and I love you."

"A prince loves me! Oh me, oh my, what a fairy tale!"

If there weren't cats flailing about our feet, I would've shown her exactly how much I loved her. Instead, I just kissed her again and hoped against hope that this happiness would actually last.

CHAPTER FIFTEEN

In the flurry of engagements we had scheduled, I nearly forgot about Connor's threats. Laurent updated me with any pertinent information regarding the palace's investigation and plans, but more often than not, there wasn't much information to convey.

The palace had managed to contact Connor and to pressure him to give up on his plans, threatening serious legal consequences should he publish anything that would damage the reputation of the royal family. Publishing something truly libelous would result in steep fines and potential expulsion from Salasia itself.

But when the two weeks passed and nothing happened —no photos published, no stories leaked—I felt like a could take a deep breath. When a third week passed without incident, it seemed as though Connor had decided that it wasn't worth facing the strength of the palace's lawyers to get his money.

Now, Niamh and I were welcoming a group of doctors, nurses, and other medical professionals to the palace as a thank-you for their contribution to the Salasian people and to the country itself. It was a rather standard engagement, standing in queue and shaking hands with person after person, chatting with all of them briefly to hear their stories.

Niamh stood by my side and shook hands with a smile on her face, French passable enough now to have simple conversations with the attendees. She'd come a long way since we'd first married; now she seemed at ease, whereas before she'd always seemed as though she'd rather be anywhere else. She chatted and laughed, engaging a group of nurses in a conversation about the cats. When she caught me looking, she shot me a bright smile.

The entire day went as scheduled and was rather dull. I had to stifle a yawn near the end of the engagement, Niamh's eyes laughing when she saw me looking bored.

"I can't believe you were bored listening to the podiatrist talk about all of his patients with toe fungus," said Niamh in a low voice.

"I'm not sure which was worse: talking about toe fungus or plantar warts."

"I missed the warts bit."

"You really didn't miss anything, I promise you."

Niamh excused herself to use the restroom, leaving me to the continue mingling. When Niamh hadn't returned after ten minutes, I went to Laurent, quietly asking where she'd gone. Laurent assured me he'd have a servant see where she could've gone. I knew she wouldn't simply have left with no intention of returning without telling me, unless something had happened.

Laurent found me, taking me to a corner where we could have some measure of privacy.

"Where is she? Is she all right?" I demanded.

"Your Highness, it must've happened within the hour." Laurent pulled out his phone and showed me. "I'm so sorry, sir."

The photos of Niamh topless were splashed across a trashy tabloid's website. I swiped through the photos, not sure why I needed to look at each and every one. Maybe I hoped that my rage could burn through the phone screen and disintegrate the photos right then and there.

"Fuck. Fuck, fuck, fuck."

"I concur, sir," said Laurent.

I shoved the phone toward him, stalking away. When a servant tried to approach, he saw my expression and promptly backed away.

I wished I'd strangled Connor Gallagher when I'd had the chance. Why had I been so stupid as to think he would give up? That he'd have some change of heart and realize what an utter piece of shit he was? I'd been a fool, and my wife would pay the price for it.

When Niamh reappeared, though, she was all smiles when she saw me. She must not know yet. When she saw my expression, she shot me a confused look.

"You look like someone just up and died," she said jokingly.

"Where were you?"

"I was talking to some of the guests. I didn't know I'd been gone that long. Were you looking for me? I'm sorry."

I had my hand on her elbow. I was trying to guide her

away, to keep any of the media from talking to her, but the crowd was too dense and too many people wanted our attention. Even with Laurent trying to assist us, it felt like we were swimming against a current in the middle of the ocean.

"Your Highnesses! Do you have any comment on the current *situation*?" a journalist said in French. He then repeated himself in accented English to Niamh.

"Situation? That's a weird way to refer to this." She turned toward the journalist and replied in French, "We are having a lovely time."

"Oh, how amazing you are, to keep your head up, in a time like this! Such a strong woman you are, madam," said the journalist.

A few other journalists and photographers had begun to join our group, making it nearly impossible for me to get Niamh out of her. I would have to elbow my way through, which would only cause a spectacle, something these vultures loved.

"I'm aware that I'm amazing," said Niamh lightly, "but I'm not sure I deserve that much praise for shaking a bunch of doctors' and nurses' hands today. I'm also sure my husband is much better at shaking hands than I am."

That remark elicited a few chuckles, but I could see anticipation on the media's faces, like sharks out for blood.

"Thank you for attending. My wife and I appreciate all of your support," I said as I began to move away from the group toward an exit to the kitchens.

"Those photos, though! I hope you will punish whoever published them."

I didn't know who said the words, but I wanted to punch them. I wished we did have a dungeon, and I could lock away anyone who thought it was appropriate to tell my wife this awful news in front of a crowd like this.

Niamh, clever as she was, didn't take the bait. "I believe my husband is about to rip off my arm, he's so hungry."

The resulting laughter allowed us a moment to get away. I pulled Niamh into a room that Laurent had unlocked and was now guarding from any prying eyes or curious ears.

Niamh already had her phone out. It took less than ten seconds for her to discover what that journalist had meant. I watched as her face paled, her mouth trembled.

She showed me. "Did you know?" Her voice was a hoarse whisper. When I didn't answer right away, she said, more harshly, "Did you know?"

"I found out only minutes before you did."

She started to look at the photos, which I knew would only make things worse.

"Niamh, don't torture yourself. We'll get this taken care of and sue the person who did this," I said. "I promise."

"How did they even get these? I think I would've noticed some creep hanging out in the bushes around the pool."

"They took these from some distance."

Niamh sighed and finally put her phone away. "I can admire their persistence, at least."

I hated how she was trying not to sound overly emotional, that she was trying to keep the subject light. I wanted her to yell; I wanted her to throw her phone at the wall. But she just smiled, albeit a wobbly smile, and shrugged.

"Doesn't every famous person deal with shit like this?" She spread her fingers. "I guess this just shows how famous I really am now."

"Niamh—"

"Don't. Don't feel sorry for me. I'm this close to losing my fucking mind, so if I just act like it doesn't matter…" She took in a shuddering breath. "Don't be nice to me right now."

"I'm not going to act like this isn't a fucking huge invasion of privacy or that I'm not so angry I could cheerfully murder the person behind this."

Something in my tone caught Niamh's attention. She narrowed her eyes. "What aren't you saying? You seem especially pissed about this."

"You're my wife!"

"No, like it's personal." Niamh stepped closer, analyzing my face. "You knew about this way before today. Is that it?"

I considered lying and then decided against it. "Yes, I knew." I nearly disclosed that it involved her father, but I held back. I didn't know why. Was I afraid of her reaction? Or that she'd finally get angry at someone —namely, *me*?

"You knew, and you didn't tell me. How long, Olivier? How long did you know these photos existed and decided I shouldn't be aware?"

When I didn't give an exact number quickly enough, Niamh shook her head, scoffing. "Wow, that long. Pretty much right after our honeymoon, I'm guessing. Or were we still at the villa when you found out?"

That anger I was expecting from her filled her voice. I clenched my fists.

"I was protecting you," I said, trying to keep my tone level, calm. "I knew of the photos, but our lawyers were handling it."

"They were photos of me! Photos of my bare tits! I had a right to know that I'd been fucking violated!"

"And what could you have done about it? We didn't know who was behind it. We were handling it as we handle any kind of photo that we don't want published. You aren't a private citizen anymore—"

Niamh laughed hollowly. "I'm well aware of that. Nobody was taking pictures of me topless from miles away before I married you."

I flinched. "I'm sorry," was all I could think to say.

"For what? Not telling me or putting me in this situation in the first place?"

"You agreed to this marriage. You could've let your brother handle everything, but you chose not to. That was your choice, Niamh. Don't lay that at my feet."

"Of course I'm going to protect my brother, my family!"

"Just like I've been protecting my family, including you."

We stared at each other, clearly at an impasse. Niamh's cheeks were red, and tears were in her eyes now.

Her voice hitched as she said, "I can't do this. You're not going to make me feel sorry for you when I'm the one who's been fucked with. I'm the one who's been humiliated, not you."

I tried to take her hands, but she pushed me away. "That's why I was trying to protect you. I didn't want you to feel like this. Don't you understand?"

"You can't keep me in a bubble, either. I'm not a little girl who needs to be sheltered. I'm a grown woman who deserves to know the truth, because you respect me. It's as simple as that."

"I do respect you. I love you."

She shook her head. "Stop. Please stop. You can't love somebody if you don't respect them." She kept shaking her head, the tears falling now. "Why do I get the feeling you weren't protecting me, so much as continuing to protect yourself and your reputation? Those photos being leaked makes the entire royal family look bad."

"For the love of God, Niamh—"

"No, no, I can't do this." She hurried off, crying, and although I wanted to chase after her, I knew it was futile.

I sat down heavily on a chair and put my head in my hands. I didn't hear when Laurent approached. I only noticed his presence when he cleared his throat.

"Celia escorted the princess to her quarters, Your Highness," he said quietly. "She'll make certain no one sees them."

I sighed. "Thank you."

Then to my surprise, he reached down and gingerly squeezed my shoulder. "It'll work out, sir."

"Will it? Do you have a crystal ball that tells you as much?"

"As convenient as that would be, I do not. But I do know that if two people care enough about each other, they'll make their way back to each other. I have confidence in that."

"If only I had that same confidence, Laurent."

CHAPTER SIXTEEN

The scandal of the photos exploded. Not only was it late in the summer and there was little news for the media to publish, but I'd always known that a certain percentage of the public had been waiting for Niamh to screw up like this.

I'd hoped that there would be more sympathy, but when Laurent showed me multiple news stories blaming Niamh for being topless on her honeymoon, I had to tell him to stop showing them to me.

As for Niamh, she'd begun to sleep in her bedroom again. When I'd knocked on her door the evening after the revelation, she'd refused to talk to me. I'd had to bribe Celia to get a note to my wife, as she wasn't answering calls or texts, either.

I couldn't sleep. I'd gotten used to Niamh sleeping beside me, the way she hogged the bedcovers, or how she tended to sprawl across the bed and take up more than three-quarters of it. I'd often end up sleeping on the edge of the mattress. But I hadn't minded, because she'd been in bed with me, and any discomfort was worth that.

A part of me didn't regret not telling Niamh about the existence of the photos. If we'd succeeded in making them disappear, she would never have had to feel like this. I'd still have my happy, free-spirited wife instead of this ghost who haunted my thoughts and dreams.

Although the photos were taken down from the original website, they popped up on more websites. When one website was successfully cowed to take them down, another five reposted them. It was an endless game of whack-a-mole, except it involved a continuous loop of violation against my wife.

I hated feeling so powerless. I hated that I'd made my wife cry. Most of all, I hated Connor Gallagher, and I wished him to the deepest pit of hell for all of this.

And now, my father wanted a *conversation*. Both of my parents had been debriefed about the situation long ago, although I'd never spoken to them about it directly, until now.

My father sat behind his desk in his office. There was a table with sandwiches and drinks, but they looked untouched.

Ever since my mother had revealed more about my biological father, I'd had little interaction with Étienne. Distance had grown between us. Seeing him now, I felt more disconnected from him than ever.

"Olivier," he said, rising. "Thank you for coming to see me."

I sat down, hating the formality of this strange meeting.

If my father wanted us to repair our relationship, he wasn't going to do it treating me like this.

"How is Niamh?" was my father's first question.

I looked at him surprise. "She's…" I struggled to find the right word. "Upset. And angry."

My father nodded. "Of course. Please know that your mother and I want her to know we support her. I can't imagine how she feels right now." His gaze softened. "How are you?"

"I'm fine. Better than Niamh, at any rate."

"You can't blame yourself. These things happen, unfortunately. As the royal family, there will always be people wanting to profit off of our pain or discomfort."

I gritted my teeth. "They violated my wife. It's more than just some embarrassing snafu that can be waved away."

"You're angry."

I laughed, but it was a bitter sound. "I'm angry? Of course I am. I couldn't protect her from this. I told myself that I'd do everything in my power to keep her safe, and I failed. So, yes, I'm angry—at myself."

"You love her."

Christ, I did not want to have this conversation, especially with my father. I looked away from the concern in his face. "My feelings about her are irrelevant."

"That's a complicated way of saying yes." He smiled gently. "I want you to know that despite everything, I still love your mother. I've always loved her."

I stared at him in surprise. "Why? She was pregnant with another man's child."

"I met your mother when she was in a desperate situation, yes. She was already pregnant, and her family was pressuring her to 'go away for the summer,' if you know what I mean."

"They were pressuring her to give me up?"

"Very much so. According to your mother, they'd already had another family wanting to adopt you. She, however, wanted to keep you. She loved you very much, and always has, despite what you might think now."

Apparently, my father had asked for this meeting to discuss the most awkward subjects possible. I tried to find something to say to lighten the mood. I wished Niamh were here. She'd know what to say to get everyone laughing.

"Your mother told me everything—about Gaspard, about how he'd abandoned her, the baby—and I knew I had to protect her. So, I offered to marry her. She accepted."

I shook my head, incredulous. "I wouldn't find this story so difficult to believe if you weren't the heir to the Salasian throne. Why accept another man's child, knowing that if the truth were discovered, that child would never inherit? Why put him or her in that situation?"

My tone turned harsh, and I realized that I was still angry at my parents. Not only for keeping the truth from me, but for thinking that their decisions would have no consequences whatsoever.

"I was in love." My father shrugged. "I was young, and, I'll admit, stupid."

"You were older than I am now," I pointed out.

"Stupidity tends to occur regardless of a person's age." He folded his hands. "And I knew, too, that this would be my only chance to be a father. I never told you this, but I'm sterile. I contracted the mumps as a young boy, and unfortunately…" He grimaced. "There was no hope that I would ever have children."

"And you kept this a secret? How?"

"Your grandfather did, yes. I was the only heir, and there was still hope that perhaps I could sire a child. Nothing is one hundred percent, of course. Considering your mother never became pregnant again after we married and you were born, the doctors were correct."

I had to stand up. The room, despite its size, suddenly felt too small.

"Is that everything?" I demanded. "Have you finally told me all of the secrets surrounding my birth? Because at this point, I'm half-expecting you to tell me I was actually dropped at your doorstep by the stork."

"No storks or other fowl were involved in your birth, I can assure you of that."

I snorted. "Well, that's comforting." I pushed my fingers through my hair. "What you and Mother did…I don't understand it. I'll never understand it, when you knew what would happen if it were discovered. It didn't seem like a risk worth taking to me."

"Love is a risk that's always worth taking."

"You sound like a greeting card now."

My father smiled. "Maybe, but it's true. That's what I asked you about Niamh. If you love her, you'll do anything to keep her." He added softly, "Don't drive her away for a throne and a future that can't love you back."

"So I should simply abdicate and let Connor Gallagher sit on the throne?" I shook my head. "No, I will never let that happen. I will never let the royal family fall into his hands."

"You might not have a choice." My father rose and placed a hand on my shoulder. "Take it from me, son: duty might seem more pressing, but it won't keep you warm at night, either. Love, though? It will."

I stared off into the distance. "Does Mother even love you? Or has she ever loved you?"

"In her own way, yes."

"That's enough for you?"

"It has been, but I hope you'll have more than that. I hope that you'll have all the love that your mother and I didn't have in our lives."

CHAPTER SEVENTEEN

In desperate need of keeping my mind off of the disaster that was my marriage, I randomly decided one morning to go riding. I hadn't spent much time with any of the horses in some years, as my princely duties took up more and more of my leisure time.

I'd always enjoyed riding as a child. After the debacle when I'd ridden off and gotten lost for hours as a child, though, I'd stopped riding. It had soured the sport for me, and then life had taken hold and I'd stopped entirely.

My mare, Juliette, nickered softly as we started down the lane that led to a trail that meandered through a forested area five kilometers outside Saint Henri. It was a beautiful, late summer day. With the dappled sunshine following just me and my horse, I could almost imagine everything was fine.

I could almost imagine that my wife was speaking to me. That there weren't dozens of stories, online and in print, about those titillating photos of her bare breasts. That there weren't other stories about how my parents were shunning

Niamh (untrue), that I was shunning Niamh (ridiculously false), or that Niamh was considering going back to the United States (status: unknown).

I kicked Juliette into a canter. My thighs burned, reminding me of how strenuous riding was and that it'd been a while since I'd done it. I'd probably be bow-legged tonight, I thought wryly.

The trail meandered through the forest, eventually reaching a tiny village that was known for its vineyards and wine tastings. It was an idyllic place, somewhere you could almost believe was untouched by modern technology. I was surprised when my phone still had service there.

The locals recognized me immediately. One of the most famous winemakers came to greet me outside his restaurant, beaming.

"Your Highness, we are honored to see you here of all places!"

"Is there a place I can leave my horse?"

"I can have it taken care of, sir. Please, come inside for a wine tasting. I have a new merlot that I'm certain you will love."

A young man took Juliette toward a nearby stable—horses weren't uncommon methods of transport in these parts—and I followed the vineyard owner into the restaurant. It wasn't yet open, so there was only staff readying for dinner later that day.

The vineyard owner, who told me his name was Francois, brought five different wines to try. I was sipping the third one, a delicate white wine that was especially floral in its scent, when I heard a commotion outside.

Francois bustled over. "What could that be? I hope it is not Gerard again. His wife has kicked him out of the house so many times now that we've lost count. He always comes here afterward, usually barefoot and sometimes without even a shirt on."

"His wife kicks him out without letting him dress?"

"Well, she often throws his clothes and shoes outside along with him. Sometimes they land in the mud."

The commotion continued, the voices getting louder outside. "Sounds like a bad deal for Gerard," I said.

"The last time his wife threw him out, he'd brought home a—" Francois cleared his throat. "Well, not a woman you'd want your husband to bring home. Apparently, the police were called because his wife tried to set the bed on fire with the two lovers in it."

My lips twitched. "What an upstanding citizen he is."

As I wondered if Gerard had gotten caught again with another woman, I heard a man yelling in English. Most notably, English with an Irish tinge. The hairs on the back of my neck rose.

And then Liam Gallagher, angry, sweaty, and as big as a bear, burst through the entrance to find his prey: me.

"You," said Liam, growling like I'd imagine a mother bear would growl if you got near her cubs. He approached, his finger pointed at me. "*You.*"

"Liam, for the love of God—" Liam's wife Mari flew in behind him. Her red hair was surprisingly disheveled. I'd never seen her look anything but immaculate for the week they were here attending the wedding.

I rose. Francois fluttered back to me, and I told him in French, "It's all right. He's my brother-in-law."

Francois looked at Liam then looked back at me. Then he just said in a whisper, "Godspeed, Your Highness."

I could feel the gazes of the waitstaff on all of us. I approached Liam slowly.

"Olivier," said Mari, shoving at Liam and failing, "I'm so sorry about this. I told Liam we could wait for you to return, but he refused."

"I wasn't going to sit all day drinking tea, waiting for this arsehole to come back."

"What have I done now? You've been here all of five minutes," I pointed out.

"What have you done? Are you bloody serious?" Liam's expression turned grim. "You promised me that you'd keep my sister safe. But you failed. And you're just sitting around, drinking wine, not a care in the world. Did you even care what's happened to Niamh? Or was it just par for the course around here?"

A cloud of red passed over my vision. "You don't know what you're talking about. You have no fucking idea what we've been through lately, what she's been through."

Liam folded his arms across his chest. "Enlighten me. Tell me what you've done that proves to me you've been a decent husband."

"I don't have to prove anything to you. Jesus Christ." I shook my head, incredulous at this man's audacity. "Your sister is an adult. I doubt she'd be happy if she knew you flew all the way here to meddle in her relationship."

"My sister is young and she's my *sister*. I'll always protect her."

Mari said, "I told him this idea was stupid, coming here.

But when he insisted, I came along to make sure he didn't do anything totally stupid."

"I'm not sure even you could prevent him from doing something stupid," I said wryly.

"Don't talk about me like I'm not here. Fucking hell." Liam went to the table where I'd been wine-tasting and slugged back one glass after another. "Is there any whiskey in this place?"

"It's a vineyard, you dumbass, not a distillery," I said.

Liam scowled. "You really have a death wish, don't you?"

"Liam, you can't murder your brother-in-law." Mari heaved a sigh, turning to me. "I'm sorry. I really did try to stop him."

"You were just as pissed as me. I distinctly remember you saying that you'd love to run Olivier over with your car," said Liam.

I raised an eyebrow. "Is everyone in Niamh's family wanting to murder me?"

"I can't believe Niamh herself hasn't murdered you." Liam was stalking around the restaurant. Waitstaff hurried out of his way, one girl turning as white as a sheet as she scurried into the back. Another waiter made the sign of the cross. Considering the dark look in Liam's eyes, I couldn't blame him. He did look rather demonic.

"How did you even find me?" I asked.

"We followed you." Liam picked up a bottle of wine from the bar and then went behind it to search for a bottle opener.

"Christ, the security lately has been abysmal," I

muttered. Then I looked at Mari; she had spatters of mud on her ankles. She was also wearing a skirt and heels.

"Did you *walk* all this way?" I said.

Mari sighed. "I made Liam give me a piggyback ride for most of the way. He also owes me a new eyeshadow palette for putting me through all of this. Actually, he owes me more than one. Maybe three."

When she shot her husband a glare, he looked a little cowed. "Whatever you want, princess."

I snorted. Clearly, Liam was only as terrifying as his wife allowed him to be. I had a feeling if she demanded it, he'd kneel down and kiss her feet. It said a lot that he wouldn't listen to her in this instance. He must really, really want kill me.

Normally, the thought that someone wanted to kill me would scare me. But this entire tableau was so absurd that I could only find it darkly amusing.

Poor beleaguered Francois was watching this ridiculous scene in abject horror. When Liam failed to find a bottle opener, he slashed the bottle open with a knife, spilling the red liquid all over his hands and the floor.

"Oh my God, the merlot!" Francois wrung his hands. "How could you—!"

Since Francois was speaking in French, Liam merely raised an eyebrow.

I sighed. To Francois, I said, "We'll pay for everything, of course. Please include a cask of the merlot for the palace. I'm sure my father would enjoy it immensely."

Francois looked somewhat mollified, but disgust filled his face when he saw Liam drinking directly from the bottle.

"Monster!" he muttered in French. To me, he added, "Should I call the police, Your Highness?"

I considered saying yes. Seeing Liam hauled to jail to stew would be amusing, but then again, I didn't need an additional scandal.

I shook my head. "I'll take care of this."

I was about to ask my in-laws to go outside, so at least no more merchandise would be destroyed, when my wife entered the restaurant and said, "What the ever loving *fuck* are you doing here?"

I honestly couldn't tell if she was referring to me, to Liam, or even to Mari.

"Niamh—" I said, approaching her.

But she only had eyes for her brother. "Did you break that bottle of wine? How old are you again?" She whirled on Mari. "And you got on a plane with him willingly? Without so much as texting me to let me know you were going to show up on our doorstep?"

Mari grimaced. "I'm sorry, Niamh. Liam insisted. And we scheduled the trip so quickly that it pretty much escaped my mind to text you."

"Don't get on Mari. This is all on me." Liam rounded on his sister.

In that moment, I had time to see how similar they looked. Both had dark hair and those blue eyes. But while Niamh was slight and of average height, her brother was tall and muscular. They both had the same stubborn look on their face, though, along with the same clenched jaw and jut of the chin. It was like they were mirrors of each other.

"Are you all right?" Niamh went to me and threaded an arm through mine.

I was so surprised that it must've clearly shown on my face. Liam's forehead creased.

"I'm fine," I said in French, mostly to piss off Liam. "Your brother makes a lot of noise."

"Yes, this is true." Niamh turned her gaze back to him. "What did you think you were going to do, coming here unannounced? Throw me over your shoulder and take me home?"

"Don't protect that sack of shite! He promised me he'd protect you, and look what happened. He should be begging you for forgiveness, yet he stands here like he's the one who's been violated—"

Niamh paled. "Will shut the hell up?" She rubbed her forehead. "You don't know anything. I told you that you had no right to meddle. How many times did I say that? But you won't listen."

"You're allowed to have concerns," I said, this time in English, "but the dynamics of our marriage are between us. Our marriage has nothing to do with you."

"Shut up, will you? I've known my sister her entire life; you've known her for less than a year. I can tell she's lost weight; she has those dark circles under her eyes that she gets when she's super stressed."

"Gee, thanks," said Niamh dryly.

"And I know you didn't marry her because you loved her."

At that, Niamh flinched. I let go of her arm and said in her ear, "Go stand by Mari."

"What?"

"Just do it."

The moment she moved away from me and Liam, I

launched myself at Liam. I punched him square in the jaw, making him roar with fury.

"You bloody little arse-wipe!" He yelled something in Irish and took hold of me by my shirt collar.

Although he was taller and bulkier than me, I was faster. I kicked him in the shin and, before he could react, kicked him behind the knee, using his own weight against me. What I didn't consider was that he'd take me down with him.

Then we were rolling on the floor, punching, elbowing, scratching, and swearing, the sounds of Mari and Niamh telling us to stop just background noise. We rolled into a table, sending a carafe of wine bottles crashing to the floor.

Liam landed a punch to my gut; I wheezed, the breath whooshing out of me. Before he was able to get up, though, I managed to elbow him right in the solar plexus. He collapsed like a fallen oak.

We both lay on the floor, panting, bruised, and sweaty, when Niamh and Mari came to stand over us both.

Both women looked murderous.

"Are you done now?" This from Mari. She had her hands on her hips.

I heard the sound of wailing and realized it was from poor Francois. I groaned, slowly sitting up.

"Yes, are you done now?" inquired Niamh. She had a smile on her face, but there was no joy in it. "Oh, and look at that: the staff filmed everything. I'm sure it's already on Facebook."

"It's uploading," replied a young woman some meters away.

"Please be sure to tag my husband." Niamh scowled

down at me. "I want everyone to know what a fucking idiot he is."

A few people giggled awkwardly. I slowly rose to my feet, my wife making a point not to offer a hand to help me up.

"Niamh," I said. I winced, pain shooting through my hand. "Christ, is your skull made of fucking bricks?" I said to Liam.

He was also standing up now, his lip thoroughly swollen. The sight of it made me smirk.

"Let's go, Mari." Liam tried to take his wife's hand, but she slapped it away.

"You two morons can figure out your own way back. Even better, you can both ride Olivier's horse. Have fun with that."

Then our wives left us, broken glass and spilled wine everywhere, and Francois moaning and wailing as he surveyed the damage.

"I'll pay for everything," I repeated. "And then some."

"Oh, but dinner tonight, it is ruined——!"

"I'll pay for that, too." I would've handed him cash, but the royal family never carried it.

Liam pulled out his own wallet and handed Francois a stack of Euros. "Sorry," he said gruffly.

Francois's expression lightened somewhat. Then he said to me in French, "So that will be ten caskets of wine instead of one, yes?"

CHAPTER EIGHTEEN

"Do you know how to ride?" I asked Liam.

"A horse? Fuck no."

I rolled my eyes. I was tempted to ride Juliette back and let Liam fend for himself, but Niamh wouldn't be too happy about that, no matter how angry she was with her brother.

And of course, Niamh and Mari had driven back, leaving us stranded.

"Then I guess we'll have to walk back," I said.

Liam shot me a dark look. "I'm not walking back with *you*."

"Do you even know how to get there? Because if you get lost and slowly starve to death in the forest, I won't be upset about it."

"I have a fucking phone." When Liam pulled out his phone to discover that service was spotty out here, he cursed. And cursed. And then cursed again.

It would be funny, if I weren't bruised and if it weren't still hard to breathe. It would be funny, if my wife weren't angry with me and probably building a guillotine with my name on it right this moment.

"We could ask for a ride," I said, "but considering we just made poor Francois weep, I doubt anyone would be so charitable."

Liam turned and began to stalk toward an unsuspecting townsfolk. Before Liam could so much as say *s'il vous plaît, monsieur,* the terrified man ran in the opposite direction.

Sighing, Liam just said, "Let's go."

Normally, I wouldn't mind walking the five kilometers to where my driver was waiting for me, but doing it with my brother-in-law was another thing entirely.

We were both walking slowly. Liam winced when he stepped on a rock and then growled when he nearly face-planted into a shrubby bush when he tripped over a tree root.

"Try not to break your neck," I said, rather jovially.

"I'll break your neck, you smarmy bastard."

I let the insult pass, even as I imagined punching him again. I rather hoped he would break his neck and I could just leave him here to rot.

"What did you hope to accomplish, coming all the way here? Because as it looks to me, you've only made the situation worse," I said.

Liam was silent a long moment. "I didn't know what I wanted to accomplish. I just wanted to make sure my sister was all right."

"So you flew halfway across the world on a whim?"

"It wasn't a whim. I did it because I saw all over the Internet what the world was saying about your wife. About my *sister.* And how photos of her—" Liam coughed. "Anyway, pictures of her were everywhere, pictures that I knew would humiliate her. So I fucking flew all the way here to figure out how the hell this happened."

I stopped in my tracks. It took all of my self-control not to deck him. "I never wanted this to happen. I did everything in my power to prevent it, but sometimes, even the royal family can't stop shitty people from making money from our misery. It's part of the deal. Niamh knew that when she married me."

Liam thrust a finger in my face. "You promised me. You said nothing would happen to her."

I slapped his hand away. "Everything *within my power.*" Then I spat out, "Your father did this. Connor Gallagher. Not me, you arrogant dick. If you want to blame someone, blame the person who shares half of your DNA."

Liam stared at me. I watched as a myriad of emotions crossed his face, until his expression shuttered close.

"You're sure?" he said.

"He threatened me himself. So yes, I'm sure."

I heard a low growl, and for a moment, I wondered if there were actually bears in this patch of forest. But it was Liam, and the sound grew and grew. Then Liam was pummeling a tree trunk, the tree shaking from the force. Leaves fell around him.

I just waited. Soon enough, he was shaking his hand, and I could make out blood on his knuckles.

"Do you feel better?" I asked.

"No."

We didn't say much after that. But Liam's anger toward

me seemed to have diffused somewhat. At the very least, he wasn't threatening to end my life.

We were only a kilometer from our destination when he said quietly, "Did Niamh tell you about what happened to us?"

"With your father?"

Liam nodded tightly. "I have no lost love for that piece of shite. You telling me that? It doesn't surprise me. A man who abandons his family without a word is one who'd try to make a buck off of them, too, even in the worst possible way."

"What's your point, Gallagher?"

"My point is that I've been the one to take care of Niamh since she was a baby. Our mam died when she was really young. I was basically her father. I was the one who took her to school, who made sure she ate her carrots. I bought her clothes and brushed her hair." He smiled, a far-off smile. "Couldn't ever French braid for shite and still can't do it with two daughters of my own now."

Liam sighed. "And when I married Mari, we were stupid about it. We got drunk and married in Vegas after only knowing each other a few days. I knew that if my grandda found out, he'd keep Niamh's inheritance from her. So Mari and I played it like we were really in love."

"You don't love your wife?"

"I love her *now*. It just took a second, and for me to get my head out of my arse. Keep up, Prince.

"But what I'm saying is I'd do anything for Niamh. And of course, for my wife and my daughters. The thought that I was thousands of miles away and I couldn't keep Niamh safe…"

I hated that I understood his frustration and his worry, because it humanized him. It was easier to see him as a bonehead with all of the subtlety of a bull in a china shop.

"I love your sister." I stopped, facing Liam now. "Like you, I didn't at first, but I do now. And you need to know that this entire thing…" I struggled for the right words. "It's been agony, seeing her hurt, knowing that I failed. Whatever anger you hold toward me is nothing in comparison to the anger I have at myself."

Liam folded his arms. He assessed me, but I was used to people assessing me. I'd been assessed my entire life.

"You love her?" he asked.

"Yes."

"Does she know this?"

"Yes."

He grunted. "Okay."

I waited. Then: "That's it? That's all you have to say after nearly beating me to a pulp?"

"You're fine. You're walking, nothing's broken."

"As far as we know. I could have internal bleeding."

Liam guffawed. "If only I were so lucky." He slung an arm over me and gave me a sideways hug. "Does Niamh love you back?"

"Christ, are we really going to act like teenage girls at a slumber party right now?"

"Answer the question."

"Yes, she does. Happy?"

"No, because you don't deserve her, but I'll live with it."

I decided that that was the best response I was going to get out of my brother-in-law. By the time we returned to the car, dusty and disheveled, I had to persuade my driver not to take me to the hospital after he saw my bruised jaw.

"No, he hasn't kidnapped me," I assured my driver. "This is my brother-in-law."

My driver's eyes widened. "And he beat you, sir? What kind of a family gathering is this?"

"An Irish one," I said wryly, leaving my poor driver to gape at me in confusion as I let Liam into the car with me.

BY THE TIME I'd showered and had Laurent bandage my wounds—he was horrified when he first saw me—I went to the cat room to find my wife. There, I found her with not only the cats, but two children who were currently pouncing on each other.

Portia and the kittens were watching from a safe distance high above as the young girls pounced, hissed, and pounced again.

"Where did you find more cats?" I asked. "These ones seem feral."

"Girls, can you stop for a second? These are my nieces, Fiona and Dahlia. This is my husband, Olivier."

I'd briefly met both girls at the wedding, but I'd been so distracted that I'd honestly forgotten their faces right afterward. Fiona was red-haired and tall like her mother, while Dahlia was dark-haired like her father. They both looked like they'd happily set the palace on fire and laugh with glee as it burned.

I held out my hand. "Nice to meet you. Again."

Fiona took my hand. Dahlia just hissed and ran to hide in one of the cat tunnels. She almost fit inside it.

"Sorry, they're pretending to be cats." Niamh pointed out two bowls of milk. "You missed dinnertime."

"What a shame. How old are they again?"

Fiona's nose crinkled. "You can *ask* me. I'm right here."

"Fi, don't be rude," said Niamh.

"Well, he can. Ask me."

"How old are you, then?" I asked.

"I'm four. Dahlia's two. She talks but it's hard to understand. I'll tell you if you don't know what she's saying."

"I would appreciate that," I said seriously.

Dahlia began to wiggle out from the tunnel, only to discover that it had gotten stuck around her shoulders. Standing up, she was now half tunnel, half girl. A loud whine began to emanate from the tunnel.

"Neeeeeeeeeev, help meeeeeeeee!"

Niamh went over to get the tunnel off, but it wouldn't budge. Dahlia started crying.

"Here, you hold her and I'll pull it off," I said.

As Niamh held Dahlia by the waist, I pulled hard. After a moment of resistance, I yanked the tunnel off of her.

Dahlia was red-faced, her hair full of static electricity. She was crying in loud, gulping sobs.

"It's okay! You're fine." Niamh soothed her and gave her a tight hug. She gave me a look that said she was trying very hard not to laugh.

"Dahlia gets stuck in a lot of places," Fiona informed me. "Once she got stuck in between those stair things."

"Banisters?"

Fiona shrugged. "Yeah, I guess. Mom had to use butter to get her head out."

Dahlia had stopped sobbing, with a few more tears eking out. Then within a few minutes, she was back to trying to climb the cat tree to get to the cats.

"Thanks for helping," said Niamh to me, her lips twitching. "They're kind of a handful."

Now, Dahlia was sitting on the lowest arm of the tree. The trio of kittens were crouched down on the top nest, probably hoping the little girl couldn't see them.

"Dahlia, no." Niamh grabbed her niece before she toppled the tree over. "You'll break your arm and guess who'll get in trouble? Me."

I picked up a feather wand toy that I'd seen Niamh use with the cats. I began to wave it in the kittens' direction. They were soon focusing on its movement, swiping at it and trying to bite it midair.

This was enough to hold Fiona and Dahlia's attention, especially when I handed Fiona the wand and she began waving it around. The girls giggled as Mercedes nearly toppled out of the nest, grabbing onto the rope-covered pole and climbing back up to resume playing.

Watching the girls with Niamh, I had the strangest feeling that I was watching her with our own children. The thought sent a surge through me. It was simultaneously terrifying and exhilarating.

I could tell that Niamh would be an amazing mother. She was fun yet attentive, not getting angry even when Dahlia was being obstinate. And her nieces clearly adored her.

Guilt hit me then. I'd taken her away from her family without a second thought. She'd told me she was homesick, but I'd arrogantly believed that cats and cars, along with seducing her as often as possible, would keep her occupied.

Would you let her go, if she wanted to leave?

I didn't want to consider my own answer to that question.

"I'm sorry for what happened earlier," I said quietly to Niamh after Celia had collected the girls. "I shouldn't have punched your brother."

"I'm still mad about it. You were both idiots, rolling around on the floor. But I can't blame you for it, either. He had it coming."

"Have you spoken with him yet?"

She shook her head. "I'm too pissed at him right now."

Portia came over and settled in Niamh's lap, her rump going up as Niamh petted her.

"Are you going into heat again? Great timing, Portia," she said to the cat.

Portia just trilled and lifted her butt higher.

"Liam still treats me like I'm a little kid," she said to me. "I told him to mind his own business, but he not only didn't listen to me, he got on a plane to fuck everything up."

"I'm not going to defend him."

She snorted, shaking her head. "Everything's just a big mess."

I wished I could tell her it would go away, but that would be a lie. We both knew this scandal wouldn't blow over any time soon. And unfortunately, we also knew that it could happen again.

I wanted to ask if I could come to Niamh's room that night, but Mari came into the cat room. Seeing us, she said quickly, "Oh, I didn't know you were here, Olivier—no, Your Highness. Sir? Crap, what should I call you?"

"Olivier is fine."

Niamh set Portia on the floor. "Just don't let Laurent hear you. I'm pretty sure he keeps track of every instance where someone doesn't address his precious prince correctly."

"Now I'm imagining he has a journal full of just that," said Mari.

"Laurent would never be so gauche," I said with a snort.

After Niamh left to find her brother, I was going to return to my chambers when Mari stopped me.

"I know we don't know each other," she began, rather awkwardly, "and I'm probably overstepping here, so feel free to tell me to get lost."

"I can always have you thrown in the dungeon, of course."

When Mari paled, I added quickly, "I'm joking. We don't have a dungeon here."

She laughed, but I could tell she was still nervous.

"Liam is a moron, but he means well. When he found out about the photos, he went berserk. I'd never seen him like that, at least not in a long time. It was agonizing to watch," said Mari quietly.

"It's been agonizing for all of us."

"Liam would do anything for Niamh. Honestly, it's one of the reasons I fell in love with him. He's a big softie at heart. To him, family is the most important thing."

I raised an eyebrow. "I'm not sure what your point is."

"I guess I'm saying that Niamh is the same way. She and Liam—they were all the other had for a long, long time. So when Liam thought his sister was being hurt and possibly abandoned in her marriage, he thought he could rescue her, like he had when she was a kid."

I bristled at that. "She doesn't need to be rescued."

"Maybe not, but I also know that she would never admit it if she *did* need rescuing." Mari's expression was serious. "And she never would've married you if she didn't love you."

My chest tightened. I knew Niamh loved me now. But had she loved me before then? Had she married me with hopeful expectations?

"She loves you, Olivier. I see it when she looks at you." Mari leaned forward. "Don't break her heart, because you hold it in your hands. These Gallaghers—they're hard-headed and closed off, but once they give you their heart, that's it. You could crush them. It's a huge responsibility, to hold their heart like that."

I didn't know what to say, but I felt the weight of that responsibility on my shoulders. Had I taken Niamh's love for granted? I'd assumed she would stay, that she would love me, that our marriage would become real, without considering what that meant to her. What sacrifices she would be making as a result.

"I love your sister-in-law. I want our marriage to work." I swallowed. "I don't want to break her heart."

"I hope so. When you two announced your engagement after everything, we were all skeptical. Liam was certain you were marrying her just to keep your throne." Mari assessed me. "And I think he was right, but I didn't tell him as much."

"Things have changed," I said tightly.

"Well, I can't judge people on how they start their marriage, considering what Liam and I did. But I want to see Niamh happy, and so does Liam."

As solemnly as a vow, I said, "I want the same thing."

CHAPTER NINETEEN

That night, I knocked on Niamh's bedroom door and waited. It felt so reminiscent of our wedding night that I almost expected her to tell me to go away.

This time, though, she opened the door and leaned against the mantel with a questioning look. She was wearing a nightgown and nothing else, the silk strap falling down her shoulder. Her hair was down; it had grown nearly to her waist since we'd married. I wanted to wrap it around my hands as I plunged inside her.

"Did you need something?" She was smiling a little.

"You," I said simply.

"Well, that's very to the point." She glanced over her shoulder at her bed. "I was reading a book, you know. I was just about to get to the part where they bone."

I wrapped an arm around her waist. "You could get a good boning right now."

She laughed. "*Trés romantique!*"

"Did you want romance? I can go send Laurent for a bouquet of flowers. Champagne, chocolates, the works."

"Have you ever sent him to get you a box of condoms? Now I'm curious."

"That would just be cruel of me."

"That's not a no."

I pressed my forehead to hers. "I'm trying to make this sexy. Thinking about Laurent looking for condoms at the store is killing the mood, darling."

"I don't know about you, but it's getting me all hot and bothered. Do you think he'd get the magnum size just to save your ego even though he knows you don't have a Godzilla dick?"

"Niamh, for the love of God, please shut up." I was nearly about to fall to my knees, from either laughing or weeping.

"'Your Highness, do you prefer lubricated or ribbed for her pleasure'?" Niamh tugged on my hair. "Did you die?"

"Yes, I've expired. Please tell my parents it was your fault entirely."

"Oh, I'm sure they'll think that without me telling them."

I cupped her cheek in one hand and finally gave in to the urge to wrap her long hair around my other, tilting her head back for a kiss.

"Are you going to behave?" I said some moments later.

"No fucking way."

At that response, I threw her over my shoulder and carried her to the bed. She squealed in surprise, and then when I tossed her onto the bed and pulled her nightgown up to spank her, she squealed again.

"You're in a mood!" She squeaked-giggled when I spanked the other cheek.

"I'm showing my wife that she needs to submit to her husband."

Niamh just wiggled her ass in my face. "Oh okay, you do that."

That earned her a few more slaps, her ass cheeks turning cherry red. Despite her squeaks, I could tell she was getting turned on. If I dipped my fingers into her pussy, I knew she'd be wet already.

"Are you going to tie me up?" She looked over her shoulder rather hopefully.

"I didn't bring any rope. And no. I want you to be able to use your hands." The image of her tied up, waiting for me to fuck her, had my cock hardening even more. "I'm rather tempted to do it, though, and then leave you begging for me all night."

She moved so she was sitting on her knees while I stood at the edge of the bed. "You wouldn't last that long."

She delved her hand inside my pajama pants, her thumb slicking over the swollen tip of my cock. My balls drew up as she squeezed and stroked me.

"You're entirely too good at that," I rasped.

She licked my bottom lip. "I know. Your face gets all screwed up when you're about to come. It's cute."

"It is not *cute.*"

"Okay, it's super manly and intense. How about that?"

"Better." I grunted when she gave me an extra-firm squeeze. When she leaned down to take my cock inside her warm mouth, my toes curled against the carpet. She made little sounds of pleasure as she sucked and licked, and it was such an erotic scene I was probably already making that screwed-up face.

Niamh looked up at me through her dusky lashes. She gave one last suck to my cock before I pulled her up to kiss me.

I stripped her of her nightgown, touching every inch of her: her breasts, her shoulders, the indentation above her ass, behind her knees. She inhaled sharply when I pinched her nipples and when I pulled her hair to suck the skin of her tender neck.

"I'm going to have a hickey tomorrow," she said with a pout.

"That's the point." I brushed a finger over the red mark. "So everyone knows you're mine."

"Boys are so weird."

That earned her another brief spanking, which led to my hands trailing to the insides of her thighs. Parting her folds, I found her dripping, her clit swollen and begging for friction.

I flipped her over so she was on her knees on the bed. I pushed her upper body down, her ass in the air, and then plunged my cock inside her. She gasped, gripping the duvet cover hard.

I fucked her hard, the bed bouncing with each thrust. Niamh's moans became louder and louder with each stroke of my cock inside of her. I slapped her ass cheeks; I pulled her hair. I used her roughly, and she reveled in it.

Looking over her shoulder at me, her eyelids heavy, she said, "Are you going to come? Because you look like you are."

I grinned like a predator. "Not before you do. I want to feel that pussy tighten around my cock."

Niamh moaned. I thrust harder, our bodies slapping

together, the bed squeaking loudly. The sight of Niamh's bright red ass bouncing in time with me, her hair strewn over her shoulder, the sound of her gasping and moaning, was the sexiest thing I'd ever seen.

"Rub your clit for me," I said. "I know you want to."

She obeyed instantly, her fingers rubbing her swollen clit in quick circles. I watched as her entire body tensed and then felt her release slam into her. She buried her face in the duvet to muffle her scream.

Niamh was still gasping for air as I kept fucking her. I could feel sweat bead on my upper lip, my torso.

"I want you to come again," I commanded. "Keep rubbing your clit."

"No, no, I can't." She was panting hard. "Not again."

"Yes, you can. I want you to come again, Niamh."

She moaned and began to rub her clit again. This time, her orgasm started as deep shudders that ran the length of her body. She came with a sob, and the sound of her sobbing my name made me come hard inside her.

I filled her to the brim, electric shocks tearing through my limbs, my vision nearly blacking out. It took all of my strength not to collapse on top of her in a boneless heap. Instead, I managed to pull her into my arms as we lay horizontally on the bed.

I kissed the nape of her neck. When she didn't say anything for a long moment, I turned her to face me.

"Are you all right?" I looked her over, seeing the hickey on her neck. "Was I too rough?"

She shook her head. She buried her face in my shoulder, and to my horror, I saw tears in her eyes. "No, it was good. Too good."

"Too good?"

She sniffled. "I'm sorry. I don't usually cry after sex. I guess it was just super intense."

I stroked her hair, my heart pounding with anxiety. "Sweetheart, you're scaring me."

"Just give me a second."

I forced myself to let her cry a little instead of demanding her to explain. Finally, after what felt like an eternity, she wiped her cheeks and gave me a wobbly smile.

"I'm okay," she reassured me. "Really. I just felt a lot of feelings. That's all."

I brushed her tangled hair from her face. "I love you so much. You know that, right?"

"Yeah, I do." She snuggled close. "I love you, too."

The words were reassuring, but doubt still nibbled at my gut, keeping me awake deep into the night.

Liam, Mari, and their daughters stayed for a week. Liam and I found ourselves in an uneasy truce, neither acting particularly friendly toward each other but avoiding any more brawls.

Although I'd at first been surprised they'd brought their young children along, I was glad for their presence. The little girls provided a needed distraction for the adults. When conversations could've devolved into arguments, one or both of the girls managed to steer the subject in the opposite direction. Or did something that caused Liam or Mari to have to keep them from getting stuck, falling to their deaths, or breaking some priceless antique.

My parents were friendly but cold with Niamh's family. They were at a loss to watch how rowdy the girls were or how involved both parents were in their daughters' day-to-day lives. They'd grown up being raised by nannies, as I had been. Children were brought out at designated times, to show their parents some new skill like some show pony, and then promptly shuffled back to the nursery.

"They act like hellions," my mother remarked to me after the first meeting. "They need to get those girls under control."

I shrugged. "I like seeing them. They're entertaining."

"Children aren't entertainment." My mother's nose crinkled. "And they shouldn't be so *loud*."

Near the end of their visit, Niamh was spending more time with her brother, sister-in-law, and nieces than she was with me. I had to wrestle with resentment and, yes, jealousy. I had to admit that I didn't like sharing my wife's attention, not even with her own family.

But I kept that to myself, because I also knew how much her family meant to her. Preventing her from spending as much time as possible with them would only make me an enemy—again.

The morning of their flight, Liam had breakfast with just Niamh. Mari had told me that she and the girls hadn't been invited, either.

"They need some brother-sister time," she'd explained. "And without these hooligans running around and breaking things. Dahlia, please don't touch that. I don't even want to know how expensive it is."

We all said our goodbyes, Liam looking grim-faced, while Niamh looked especially melancholy. She hugged everyone multiple times, telling the girls she'd see them soon, and then as quickly as they'd arrived, Niamh's family were gone.

Niamh sat down heavily, pulling a blanket around her shoulders.

"Are you all right?" I touched her cheek. "I know it's hard to say goodbye."

"It's not that." She burrowed deeper into the blanket. "I mean, I'm sad to see them go. I hate that I'm so far away from the girls."

"I know."

"Do you? Because sometimes I don't think you get it."

I frowned. "You're going to have to explain that statement."

Blowing out a breath, she said in a monotone voice, "Liam told me. About my dad, the photos. That he was behind it all."

There was a feeling that I'd suddenly stepped not onto solid ground, but into a deep, dark hole. Cold air seemed to whoosh by me.

"Why didn't you tell me?" Niamh's eyes were hard now.

"Because I didn't want you to get hurt."

"Come on, Olivier, that's bullshit. I'm a big girl. I can take the truth. You didn't tell me my dad was involved because you didn't want me to know."

I could feel the anger coming from her in waves. I sat down, forcing calm into my voice.

"But you told my brother," she continued, "the two of you making decisions behind my back, because apparently I'm too stupid to make them myself."

"What decisions were made? None. You're seeing monsters where there are none."

"You made a decision to withhold information from me about my own dad. What else have you not told me?"

My fists were clenched, tension vibrating through me now. "I didn't tell you about your dad because I knew how hurt you'd be," I repeated.

"What else, Olivier? Tell me."

"You want to know everything? Fine." I took a deep breath. "He came here, to the palace. He wanted to see you, but I wouldn't let him. Then he blackmailed me to my face."

Niamh's face was white. She pulled her blanket closer, like she could turn it into a cocoon. "Ever since I agreed to marry you," she whispered, "I haven't had any control. Everything I say, I do, every move I make, someone else has to approve it. And now you tell me that this has been going on for months, and you didn't think I should know?"

"What good would it have done? Tell me that."

"I don't know. Maybe if I could've talked to him first, I could've kept him from doing it."

"Now you're being naive."

"Probably, but I still should have a say in my own life, in things that directly concern me." She kept shaking her head. "Sometimes I think you don't believe I can do this."

I stared at her. I felt like everything we'd been building was falling apart in front of my eyes.

"The fact that you aren't contradicting me says it all." Her smile was sad now. "You think I'm just some stupid, naive screw-up that you only married to keep your position."

"Niamh, I love you. You love me. Why are you saying this?"

"Love is one thing. But it doesn't mean much when you don't respect me, either. You think you can move me around like some chess piece, and I won't push back." She lifted her chin. "Spoiler: you can't. I might be your wife, but I'm still my own person. I won't let you, or this role or your family, force me to become someone I'm not."

"You haven't exactly been amenable to conforming to your role. You were openly antagonistic to the press in the beginning. You scoffed at taking lessons, learning French, all of it. You thought you were better than all of it."

Niamh leapt to her feet. "Fuck you, Olivier. Fuck you and the arrogant horse you rode in on. I don't need to listen to you berate me."

I rose, too. "So you're just going to run out, because things are hard? I didn't take you for being a coward."

Her shoulders stiffened. Her gaze full of daggers, she replied, "I'm leaving because I respect myself. Maybe you could try it: respecting your wife. I heard it's all the rage."

I didn't chase after her. And when she slammed the door shut, I didn't even flinch.

CHAPTER TWENTY

Niamh refused to speak with me for the next two days. On the third day, I used the same trick I'd used on our wedding night to enter her bedroom.

Only to find my wife nowhere in sight.

Celia startled when she saw me. She immediately mumbled something and tried to hurry away, but I stopped her.

"Where is my wife?"

Celia's gaze was everywhere except on my face. "I don't know, Your Highness," she nearly whispered.

"You don't know or you won't tell me?"

Celia looked like she going to burst into tears. "Sir, she forbade me from telling you. She made me swear on my mother's grave."

"Didn't you just visit your mother two weeks ago?"

Celia's chin wobbled. "It's still very upsetting to think about!" She added quickly, "Sir."

I approached her slowly, rather like you would a deer that was close to bolting. "You need to tell me where she is.

What if something happens to her and I couldn't get her help?"

"Oh, when you put it like that…"

"She can be angry with me, not you. I'll take the blame."

Celia wrung her hands. "I don't know, sir. I just don't think I can betray my mistress. She was so adamant. I've never seen her like that. It was frightening."

Steel in my tone, I said, "Tell me where she went or I'll have you fired immediately."

I instantly hated myself for the threat, especially when Celia started sobbing. After a few moments, she finally confessed that Niamh had flown to Ireland. Namely, to her grandfather's estate in Dublin.

"How did she leave without anyone seeing her?" I asked.

"I lent her a servant's uniform of mine," replied Celia, rather sheepishly. "She left late at night with no one the wiser."

I had the sudden urge to fire Celia anyway, but I had just enough self-awareness to realize that I'd be taking my anger out on an innocent party. Celia had been loyal to her employer, and I couldn't fault her for it. It was Niamh who'd put her subordinate in an untenable position.

"Don't tell anyone about this. If anyone asks, Niamh is ill and not to be disturbed," I said.

Celia curtsied. "Of course, sir."

I stalked to my own rooms, beginning to pace the length of them, racking my brain to figure out what to do.

Niamh hadn't so much as left a note. No explanation, nothing. Did she think I wouldn't care that she'd up and left? Anger, and hurt, pierced my gut. I wanted to shake her until she told me why. I'd known she was angry with me. But to run away? It wasn't like her. Niamh didn't run from anything.

I called Niamh's phone, but it went straight to voicemail. I texted her multiple messages. I told her that I just wanted to know she was all right.

I did receive a reply that simply said, *I'm fine. Please stop messaging me.*

I nearly threw my phone at the wall. I called her a second time. The phone rang this time, but it went to voicemail again. I left her a curt one that asked for her to call me when she could, all the while having a sinking feeling that she wouldn't.

Sighing, I knew there was probably only one person who would know the answer. And he was the last person I wanted to talk to.

Liam had given me his number, grudgingly telling me that since we were technically family, we should be able to contact one other. I hadn't had any intention of ever calling my brother-in-law for some fireside chat, yet not even a week since they'd returned to the States, I was calling him.

I calculated that it'd be early morning in Seattle right now. But as I listened to Liam's phone ring and ring with no answer, I had no idea who else I could try to talk to. I didn't have Mari's number, which I sorely wished I'd asked for.

"Hello?" Liam answered. "Why the hell are you calling me, Prince?"

"I wanted to ask you what your favorite color was," I snapped.

"It's blue, like your face after I punched it."

That remark made me snort, at least. Sighing, I said, "Niamh's gone to Dublin without telling me."

"And you're calling me why? Sounds like you need to talk to my sister."

"You're the one who caused this. You told Niamh about your father's involvement in the photos being released."

Liam swore in what I assumed was Irish. "You stupid shite, you didn't tell her? That's on you. I assumed you would've told her. I shouldn't have expected so much of you, then."

I gritted my teeth. "Fine. I fucked up. We fought, and we said some things."

"What things?" Liam's voice was nearly a growl.

"That doesn't matter. What I want to know is has she contacted you in the last three days?"

"No, she hasn't."

I wished I could see his expression right now to gauge if he was telling the truth.

"Look, Olivier, I don't know what you two said to each other. Frankly, I don't give a fuck. Despite what you both might think, I don't want to involve myself in some marital spat. But Niamh wouldn't leave without a legitimate reason. You must've really fucked up for her to do that."

"That I figured out for myself."

"Then you're smarter than I took you for." Liam exhaled a long breath. "Niamh didn't tell me everything about your marriage or why she agreed to it. I always knew it wasn't some great love story. But during our last conversation, she told me that a big reason why she'd said yes was to protect me, if the truth comes out.

"And I'm telling you what I told Niamh: I don't need protection. I can take care of myself, and I can take care of my family. What matters is that Niamh is taken care of, and that's what you, as her husband, need to do. She's what matters. Whatever comes, we can deal with it."

I was gripping my phone so tightly that my fingers hurt. I swallowed against the lump in my throat. "I guess I should say thank you," I said.

"You should, but you won't. Now, go get my sister, you arsehole. She loves you, although God only knows why."

I stared down at my phone for a long time after I'd hung up with Liam. I knew, before I could even think it, what I needed to do.

I'd clung to the excuse that I'd had to marry Niamh to save my throne. But did a throne matter, when love was at stake? A crown wouldn't keep me warm at night. A crown wouldn't make me happy.

I'd convinced myself that duty mattered more than anything else. But was it duty or pride? Had I clung to my birthright because accepting that it wasn't truly mine had been too bitter of a pill?

I'd wanted Niamh since I first met her in Dublin. When the chance to make her mine had come, I'd taken it, telling myself it wasn't about wanting *her*.

I'd lied to myself, I realized in that moment. Yes, I loved Niamh.

But I knew that I loved her more than I loved a crown sitting on my head.

I lurched upright. I felt simultaneously exhilarated and

exhausted. I didn't know where to start. I wanted to call Niamh again, but I had a feeling she wasn't going to talk to me unless I showed up at her doorstep.

I didn't realize I'd gone to my parents' quarters until I was outside of them. I entered without knocking, both of them having afternoon tea.

My mother blinked. "Darling, what in the world?"

"I can't keep living a lie," I said in a rush. "I'm not the heir. Not the true one. Liam, or Niamh, or some other distant cousin is. The public deserves to know that."

My mother's eyes welled with tears, while my father reached out to take her hand. He said to me, "You would put your mother through a scandal like that? Have a heart, Olivier."

"I don't want to hurt either of you, but the truth will come out eventually. You both know it will. We can either create the story ourselves or let someone else do it." I took in a shuddering breath. "Niamh is gone. She's in Dublin."

My mother was crying now, crying like I hadn't seen her before.

Going to her, I said, "I'm sorry."

She composed herself a few moments later. She suddenly looked years older. "Do what you must. I won't stop you."

"Alexandra—" said my father.

"Olivier doesn't deserve to be punished for my sins." She looked into my eyes, and I could see the steel in them. "Do whatever you must, especially when love is at stake."

I kissed her hand. "Thank you."

Returning to my quarters, I found myself going into Niamh's instead. I picked up her pillow and inhaled its scent. I didn't know if I was making the right decision, but at the very least, this burden that had hung about my shoulders would be lifted.

I wandered through her bedroom, noting that she'd left a stack of books behind, along with lip balms, bobby pins, hair ties, and other knickknacks. I flipped through one of the books, realizing that it was one of the romance novels she'd bought at a used bookstore in Paris.

I wanted to return to Paris with her and show it to her as my wife. I wanted to see her smile and moan as she ate an eclair again.

I went into her bathroom, feeling rather idiotic for wanting to mentally catalogue all of the items my wife had left behind. Her toothbrush was gone, but a new tube of toothpaste still sat on the counter. Her hair dryer was also still on the counter, along with bottles of shampoo and body wash in the shower.

She'd left in a hurry, obviously. But I wondered: had she left with the intention of returning?

I was so distracted that I accidentally kicked over a small trashcan near the toilet. Swearing, I kneeled down to pick up the mess, wondering why the trash hadn't been emptied yet. Then again, Celia had been so terrified that she'd probably forgotten.

Right there on top of the scattered trash was a pregnancy test. The result: two pink lines.

I swore. What the hell did that mean? Did that mean it was positive? Negative? Twins? Wait, one line was kind of faint compared to the other one. Did that mean "maybe, try again later?"

Shit, I didn't know what pregnancy tests told you. I

hadn't exactly had a reason to use one myself. I cursed myself for being the greatest idiot alive.

I began to sift through the trash, hoping the box was in the there, hating myself for having to dig through my wife's *trash.* At the bottom, I found the box, my heart pounding as I looked for the meaning of two lines.

Two lines: positive.

Niamh was pregnant.

My wife, pregnant, with our baby.

And she'd not only not told me, but she'd run away without so much as a goodbye.

"Laurent!" I shouted from the bathroom. "Book me a plane ticket to Dublin immediately!"

CHAPTER TWENTY-ONE

It was a strange time to be alive when I found myself barred from entering my wife's estate by a tiny slip of a maid.

"She doesn't want to see you," the maid said in a heavy Irish accent. "She explicitly told me not to let you inside."

The butler, a granite-faced man who could've been thirty or seventy, stood behind the maid and nodded.

"I need to speak with her," I repeated slowly. "It's urgent."

The maid just shook her head. "I'm sorry. It's not possible—Your Highness."

And then a door was shut in my face. Me, a prince, heir to the throne of Salasia. I had to admit that had never happened before. People tended to *open* doors for me, not close them.

Then again, Niamh had done the same thing to me multiple times now. Clenching my jaw, I went to gaze out at the vast Irish Sea, the sea air cool against my face.

I didn't understand why Niamh was literally shutting me out. Had the maid even told her I was here, in Dublin, begging to see her? Did she want me to climb some trellis to her window like Romeo? I'd be more likely break my neck with such a stunt than win Niamh's heart back.

I'd worked at the estate for a brief time, disguising myself as a gardener to gain access to the family's library. Smiling darkly, I remembered that the main gardener, Jamie, tended to leave the door from the back gardens to the kitchen unlocked.

If Niamh wouldn't let me in through the front door, I'd sneak in through the back.

On my way to the gardens, I snagged a cap that someone had left on the handle of a shovel. I also was glad that I'd worn casual clothing. Acting as though I belonged there, I opened the creaky gate to the kitchen gardens, where a variety of vegetables were growing, and got to the back door without anyone stopping me.

I need to discuss better security for this place, I thought to myself as I bounded up the servants' stairs to the second floor, where I knew Niamh had been given quarters when she'd last stayed here. I just prayed I didn't run into her maid or that butler. They looked like they'd happily tie me up and toss me into the sea without a second thought.

I nearly ran into another servant as I wandered down the long hallway. I hid in an alcove just in time for a maid to walk past without seeing me. After I'd made certain she was descending the stairs, I went straight to Niamh's door.

As I was about to knock, though, I heard voices, loud voices, and they seemed to be coming from the library.

When I heard my wife's voice, I rushed straight to the library.

I didn't think twice about bursting through those library doors or about how Niamh probably wouldn't be happy that I'd shown up unannounced. Apparently, I'd decided to pull a Liam and just fly over without so much as a note.

Niamh was standing, while there was a man sitting in an overstuffed chair. Niamh immediately spotted me, her expression shocked.

"Olivier? What—?"

I rounded on the man in the chair, knowing before I'd even seen his face who it was: Connor Gallagher.

Connor laughed when he saw me. "There he is, the prodigal prince. I told you he'd come for you, my dear. He isn't going to let what's his just wander off."

"Shut up," I said to Connor. To Niamh, I said, "Why are you talking to *him*?"

Niamh rolled her eyes. "Oh my God, is every guy in this family a drama llama? You show up here, like you're one of the Avengers, and I'm supposed to swoon at your feet?"

"What is he doing here?" I repeated, my teeth gritted.

"I asked him to come here."

I stared at her, incredulous. Connor started laughing again, until the laughter turned into an ugly cough.

"Now, can we all sit down like civilized people and talk about this?" Niamh gestured for me to sit.

I chose to stand. I didn't want Connor to try anything, even if he looked like hell. He hadn't been lying that he was dying. He looked like he was one foot in the grave already.

"As I was saying before I was interrupted," said Niamh,

"I wanted Da to come here because I wanted him to admit to my face what he'd done."

Connor snorted. "Then what? You say you forgive me and we hug it out?"

"I have no interest in hugging you. I do, however, want to give you a chance to apologize before I file charges against you." Niamh smiled grimly.

"And if I say I'm sorry, then what? You won't have me arrested?" Connor scoffed. "I don't see the point of any of this."

"No, you wouldn't." Niamh inhaled a deep breath. "I wanted to give you one last chance. Why? I don't know. Maybe I wanted to believe that my own da would feel badly that he'd hurt me so deeply. Maybe I wanted closure, closure that I knew deep down would never happen."

Niamh rose from her seat to stand over her father. "Or maybe I just wanted to tell you that I was your one last chance at family, the last person who gave a shit about you, and you destroyed it. You have nothing and no one. And you will die alone. Whether in a jail cell or your rundown, depressing flat, I don't know. Then again, I doubt your land-lord would enjoy renting to someone charged with distrib-uting what amounts to illicit photographs of his *own daughter.*

"So, it's your choice: either apologize and grovel, or you die homeless on the street or, better yet, in a jail cell."

Connor stared up at Niamh, shock written all over his face. "You have no evidence it was me."

"I have my husband's own word against you that you threatened him and me. And I'm going to guess that any judge and jury would be more inclined to believe him than someone like you."

I could tell that Connor knew he was cornered. Like a wild animal lashing out, he said with a sneer, "File whatever you want. I'll be dead before anything happens. I have only a few months to live, so think about that when you have me thrown out on the street.

"Besides," he added, looking at me, "I can still reveal the truth about your parentage. Or did you forget that? Do you really want me to tell the world that you're a bastard?"

Niamh glanced at me. I could see in her eyes that she knew that that was my decision, not hers. My heart lifted a little. If she still cared what happened to me, then there was hope for our marriage.

"I hate to burst your bubble, but I've already contacted a journalist to tell my story. The entire thing, including that my father is not actually Prince Étienne."

Niamh and Connor stared at me shock. Niamh's eyes were shining with tears, while Connor looked like he was one second away from strangling me.

"You're lying. You'd throw away everything? For what? Just to get back at me?" said Connor.

"Despite what you might believe, not everything is about you. Or me." I went to Niamh and placed a hand on her waist. When she didn't pull away, a thrill shot through me. "I'm doing it for us. Because I'm tired of living a lie."

"Olivier, are you sure? You'll lose everything," said Niamh in a tremulous voice.

"I'd rather lose my throne and my crown than lose my wife."

Connor, as was his wont, ruined the romantic moment with a scoffing noise. Getting up, he said, "He's most likely lying to lure you back, Niamh. I wouldn't believe him, if I were you."

"You're delusional if you think I'm going to take advice from *you*." Niamh pointed to the door. "You can go now. If I ever see your face here again, I'll have you arrested."

"You don't have the spine to do that. Look at you, practically falling at your prince's feet when he's lying to your face."

I grabbed Connor by his shirt collar, shaking him until his teeth rattled. "Get the fuck out of here before I toss you out myself," I warned.

Connor spat near my feet. "Go fuck yourself. You'll come crawling back to me in the end. You know it, and I know it."

I let him go, and he swore again before limping to the door. Both Niamh and I flinched when the door slammed shut.

We went to the window to watch Connor leave. He looked back at the window, and although I was sure I was imagining things, he nearly looked sad.

"Good riddance," I said. "Are you really filing charges against him?" I said to Niamh.

She sighed. "Probably. I don't know yet. It's not that he doesn't deserve it, but he's dying. Why put myself through the stress if he keels over before anything can happen?"

"I'd be tempted to do it anyway, just to see him sweat."

"I just want this to be over."

I caught her gaze, and we simply stared at each other for a long moment. Her hair was in a long braid, her face pale. She seemed thinner, too, just as Liam had pointed out.

Cupping her cheek, I said, "Why did you leave? And without saying a word to me about it?"

She swallowed. "I don't know. I just…had to get out. I felt like I was choking, like I couldn't take one step without someone telling me I was taking the wrong step. I had to go somewhere to clear my head."

"You could've still told me."

"I know." She covered my hand with hers. "It was a stupid, impulsive decision."

"And you ignored all of my messages." I couldn't keep the accusatory tone out of my voice.

"I know, I know." Niamh moved away, wrapping her arms around her waist. "I just couldn't deal with it. Sometimes, when I feel that overwhelmed, I have to completely disconnect." She turned back to me. "It's not a great coping mechanism. I know that. It's not fair to the people around me. Yet when it happens, it's almost like…I have no choice but to go hide in a cave until it passes."

"I'm not going to say I understand, but I just ask that you try to talk to me about it beforehand. Finding out you'd left, it was terrifying. I didn't know if something had happened to you. What if you'd been kidnapped, Niamh? Or had gotten hurt? You can't just run off when things get too hard."

She let out a breath. "I did tell Celia," she mumbled.

"Who you forbade from telling me."

"Considering you're here, I'm going to guess she didn't keep her promise."

"I forced it out of her. And no, telling your maid and not your husband isn't enough."

Niamh hugged me. "I'm sorry."

I let the tension in my body melt away. Hugging her close, I replied, "I'm sorry, too."

"We've both been pretty fucking stupid."

"Yes, we have."

She licked her lips. "Were you telling the truth? About revealing your secret to the world?"

"Yes. The interview is scheduled for next week. I've already disclosed what it is to the journalist so they can prepare themselves for the frenzy afterward."

"And then what happens? Does Liam inherit? Me? Will you be kicked out entirely?"

I shrugged. "I don't know. More than likely, your brother will abdicate, and then it's up to you." Going down on one knee, I took my wife's hand. "The only thing that matters is how much I love you. I want to make a life with you, Niamh. Whether that's as a royal or as a private citizen. We can live here in Dublin, or in the States, or in some shack in Siberia if you want. As long as I'm with you."

I took a deep breath. "And with our baby."

Niamh's eyes had filled with tears, but now she was blinking in confusion. "Our baby? Do you mean our future children?"

"Niamh, you don't have to lie. I found the pregnancy test. I know that you're pregnant."

Niamh helped me stand, looking at me like I'd finally lost my mind. "What pregnancy test? I didn't take a test. The last time I took one was three years ago, actually. I've been on birth control ever since. Hell, I just got my period, if that makes you feel better."

It took a long moment for my brain to compute what she was saying. "You're not pregnant," I repeated.

She shook her head. "Did you think I was? Oh my God, and I ran away, too. Did you think if I were, I wouldn't tell you?"

"I don't know."

"I'm stupid and impulsive, but I'm not cruel." She took my face in her hands. "I promise you, I'm not pregnant. I can take a test right now, if you want."

I was tempted to ask her to, but then I realized that I had no reason to distrust her. I shook my head.

"I believe you."

"Why do you sound disappointed?"

I didn't realize I was, but in that moment, I actually felt disappointed. I'd been so convinced that Niamh was pregnant, thinking about that on the flight here, that knowing she wasn't didn't make me feel relieved. It made me feel…hollow.

"I had the hope that you'd have more reason to come back if you were pregnant," I admitted.

"Oh, Olivier. You idiot. I love you. And you're willing to throw away everything for *me*. You're amazing. I don't deserve you." At that admission, her voice hitched.

I kissed her hungrily, and she kissed me with just as much enthusiasm. I tasted her tears, and I caught words of love from her mouth as I kissed her, and I knew that no matter what happened, we'd make it.

Sometime later, sitting together, Niamh in my lap, she said suddenly, "So whose pregnancy test was it?"

"Laurent's?" I joked.

Niamh's eyes widened. "Oh my God, it was probably Mari's. That sneaky little bitch. I'd noticed she wasn't drinking, but she said it was just because she didn't want the empty calories. She's totally preggo. And Liam said that he was getting snipped after two. Those liars."

I laughed. "It was probably an accident."

"Probably. And now they're going to have a third kid. Serves them right." She looked up at me. "Can you imagine three of those kids together?"

I shuddered and then thanked God that that trio of hellions would be thousands of miles away from us.

Once upon a time, a prince married a girl who didn't want to marry him. Their marriage was rocky, and the prince realized that, if he was going to keep his new princess by his side, he'd have to make the ultimate sacrifice.

The princess, touched by his generosity, accepted his heart, and he hers.

I never thought I'd have a fairy tale romance. I might be a prince, but they were fairy tales for a reason.

Niamh, of course, had proven me wrong entirely about that.

Five years after we'd married, the palace held a ball to celebrate the coronation of me and my princess as the new reigning sovereigns. My parents had decided to abdicate, feeling that their time in the spotlight had come to an end.

"We're going to be late," I said to Laurent. We were waiting for Niamh and company to arrive for our grand entrance into the ballroom.

"I heard something about a 'kitten explosion,' Your Highness," replied Laurent gravely.

"I don't even want to know what that means."

With only a minute to spare, Niamh arrived, dressed in a deep red gown that complemented her dark hair and blue eyes perfectly. She'd only grown more beautiful in the intervening years since we'd married.

She'd grown from an awkward girl who wanted nothing to do with her role to a confident princess who became immensely popular. People gravitated to her. She somehow managed to make everyone from grown men to tiny babies enamored of her.

After the news had broken that I wasn't the true heir, the scandal had been explosive. Public opinion had been split, one side wanting me to abdicate entirely, the other wanting me to stay. Strict monarchists especially had been horrified at the idea that a true Valady wouldn't be sitting on the throne.

Until the public realized that a Valady heir was closer to the throne than they thought. When Liam had refused to claim his rights to the throne, sighting that he was a "bloody American and had no business sitting on any throne," that left Niamh as the rightful heir.

And so the public had to come to terms with this upending of everything they'd been told of the future of the Salasian monarchy.

I'd slowly begun to withdraw from public life, allowing Niamh to take over. It was through her hard work that she earned the love and respect of the people. And when the palace realized that the two of us together were the biggest draw, it didn't take a genius to realize that it would be better if I became the consort to the hereditary princess of Salasia.

As for Connor Gallagher, he'd died within three months of the story breaking. We hadn't heard another word from him since that fateful day at the estate. Niamh, softhearted as she was, had attended the funeral, along with Liam. Neither sibling had shed a tear.

"Sorry, sorry, I'm here." Niamh straightened her tiara. "Is it falling off? I feel like it's falling off."

I made her stand straight so I could inspect it. "It's fine. You look beautiful."

Niamh looked me up and down. "And you look fine as hell. I'm tempted to ravish you in a closet instead of going to this thing."

"As tempting as that sounds, I don't think the attendees would appreciate it much." I leaned over and said in a lower voice, "Besides, I want to strip that dress off of you as I kiss and lick every inch of your skin."

She shivered and began to fan herself. "You rogue! Where are my smelling salts?"

The music began, and taking Niamh's gloved arm, we began to descend the staircase. My parents followed behind us, along with other important personages. Niamh's expression turned angelic, as if she hadn't just been wanting to have sex with her husband in a closet moments before.

All eyes were on my wife. If I were a jealous man, I would've felt slighted. But I didn't blame anyone for keeping their gazes on Niamh. She was radiant. Not just because she was dripping in jewels or wearing that blood-red gown. She looked like she'd stepped from another plane entirely.

"The Sovereign Prince and Princess of Salasia, Their Highnesses, Princess Niamh and Prince Olivier," a voice boomed overhead.

The two of us then stood in the center of the ballroom began waltzing. We'd practiced this dance so many times that I'd begun having dreams about it. Niamh had been especially nervous about it. She wasn't a bad dancer, but the pressure of doing it in front of a crowd had made her less confident.

Tonight, though, she floated. I mouthed the word *gorgeous* to her, and she gave me a radiant smile in return.

After our solo dance together, other couples began waltzing with us. I twirled Niamh around and then pulling her to me, saying, "Have I told you how proud I am of you?"

"Not since two hours ago, I think."

"How remiss of me."

"It's okay. I know you'll make it up to me tonight."

The night flew by in a flurry. Liam, Mari, and their three children—Fiona, Dahlia, and Henry—were in attendance. I made sure to dance with both Fiona and then Dahlia, while Niamh danced with a very somber-looking Henry. According to Mari, he'd taken his dancing duties with his aunt very seriously.

Niamh and I were eventually parted, as we conversed with all of our guests. By the time we'd found each other again, I was tempted to sneak out and go straight upstairs with my wife.

Niamh, though, was looking rather pale. I peered at her closely. "Are you all right?"

"Um, I don't know. Could you get me a glass of water?"

I had a waiter go get a glass while I led Niamh to a room nearby that was empty of guests. After the waiter had arrived with the water, I sat next to her, waiting for the color to return to her face.

"I thought I was going to faint back there." She wiped a bit of sweat from her forehead. "That was really weird."

"You never faint. Or almost faint." I touched her forehead. "Do you think you're getting sick?"

"No, no."

"I can tell Laurent to take you upstairs. You're clearly coming down with something. What if you actually faint out there?" I didn't want to take that chance.

"I'm *fine*. It was just hot in there." Niamh started to get up, but apparently it was too fast, because she was soon falling back down onto the sofa.

"Now you're scaring me. Should I take you to the hospital? We can call the palace doctor. It's late, but he could be here within the hour—"

Niamh sighed. "I don't need to go the hospital. Olivier, I'm fine." She let out a breath. "I wasn't going to tell you like this. So much for best-laid plans."

"What are you talking about?"

"I'm pregnant."

I stared at her. I'd been expecting her to say anything but that, and it took me a long moment to understand.

"Pregnant? Since when?"

"Um, since six weeks ago, I think? I just took a test a few days ago."

"And you didn't tell me?"

She waved her hands. "It's way too early, and I wanted to get a blood test done, make sure it was real, but with the ball and everything, it had to be put on hold. And then I wanted to tell you in a fun way, but I guess that's not happening now."

She looked so put out that I had to restrain myself from laughing. Sitting back down, I said, "You should've just told me."

"Yeah, yeah, looking back now that makes sense. But when do I do things that make sense? I married you, for instance."

"I'd put you over my knee right now for that."

"But I'm pregnant. Get out of jail free card! I guess pregnancy does have its benefits."

"Niamh, be serious."

"I'm never serious." But then her expression sobered. "I'm sorry. The whole thing was kind of freaking me out. You know I make jokes when something freaks me out."

I swallowed, my mouth dry. "Do you not want to be pregnant?"

"Oh no, I do. We've been talking about it for a while now, but now it's happened, it's hard to wrap my head around."

I squeezed her hand. "I feel the same way. But I'm still very, very happy about it."

"Me too. Ever since that day at the estate when you thought I was pregnant, I'd been wanting to give you a baby." She said the words shyly. "I knew it was too soon, though. I wanted to wait, yet a part of me didn't want to wait, either."

"We were trying to be responsible for once," I said wryly.

Kissing her, I told her how much I loved her, Niamh saying the same. Although I wanted her to leave the ball to rest, Niamh was adamant about staying. I kept close to her side, keeping her so well-hydrated that she complained about how many times she had to pee in her giant gown.

It was after midnight by the time we went to bed. Sitting at her vanity, Niamh was brushing her hair when I placed the antique clock in front of her.

After Connor's passing, I'd had the clock returned to the royal family. My mother had subsequently burned the letters inside.

"A gift," I said, kissing the side of her neck. "For the mother of my child."

Niamh picked up the clock. "This is your mother's. Did you steal it again?"

"No, she wanted me to give it to you. The letters are not included," I added, when Niamh opened the hidden drawer. "And I would advise that you don't place your own adulterous letters inside it, either."

Niamh snorted. "I'd keep them on a secret hard drive, duh." She turned to face me. "I love it. We've come full circle, haven't we?"

"We have. And soon, we'll have a baby of our own."

"You realize any kid we have will be a thousand times worse than all of the kittens I've fostered combined."

I kissed her nose. "You've prepared me well for that, my love."

ABOUT THE AUTHOR

A coffee addict and cat lover, USA Today bestselling author Iris Morland writes sparkling, swoon-worthy romances, including the Flower Shop Sisters and the Love Everlasting series.

If she's not reading or writing, she enjoys binging on Netflix shows and cooking something delicious.

www.ingramcontent.com/pod-product-compliance
Lightning Source LLC
Chambersburg PA
CBHW021141190726

48288CB00008B/2764